DATE DUE		

12/07

A SUMMER SMILE

A Summer Smile

Iris Johansen

WHEELER
CHIVERS

This Large Print edition is published by Thorndike Press, Waterville, Maine USA
and by the BBC Audiobooks Ltd, Bath, England
Copyright © 1985 by Iris Johansen.
Thorndike Press, an imprint of The Gale Group.
Thorndike, Star Logo and Wheeler are trademarks and Gale is a registered
trademark used herein under license.

Wheeler Publishing Large Print Hardcover.
The text of this Large Print edition is unabridged.
Other aspects of the book may vary from the original edition.
Set in 16 pt. Plantin.

LIBRARY OF CONGRESS CATALOGING-IN-PUBLICATION DATA

Johansen, Iris.
    A summer smile / by Iris Johansen.
      p. cm.
    ISBN-13: 978-1-59722-571-7 (lg. print : alk. paper)
    ISBN-10: 1-59722-571-1 (lg. print : alk. paper)
    ISBN-13: 978-1-59413-229-2 (lg. print : pbk. : alk. paper)
    ISBN-10: 1-59413-229-1 (lg. print : pbk. : alk. paper) 1. Large type books.
    I. Title.
    PS3560.O275S86 2008
    813'.54--dc22   2007042542

BRITISH LIBRARY CATALOGUING-IN-PUBLICATION DATA AVAILABLE
Published in the U.S. in 2007 in arrangement with
The Bantam Dell Publishing Group, a division of Random House, Inc.
Published in the U.K. in 2008 by arrangement with
NAL Signet, a division of Penguin Group (USA) Inc.

U.K. Hardcover: 978 1 405 64328 3 (Chivers Hardcover)

U.K. Softcover: 978 1 405 64329 0 (Camden)

Printed in the United States of America on permanent paper
10 9 8 7 6 5 4 3 2 1

DEAR READER,

As many of you know, I started my writing career in romance but I always enjoyed mixing love with high-stakes excitement. When I first wrote *A Summer Smile,* I knew the title and had only a glimmering idea that it was going to be a romance and an adventure. Sometimes it happens that way. Yet the more I thought about it, the more I realized that the title was the description of my heroine Zilah's character. She was a woman who had gone through terrible experiences, and there was no season of spring for her. Yet her strength, her belief in herself, and her ability to create a new future had given her confidence and brought her into the fulfillment of the summer of her life.

We all go through hard times and we all hope for the healing of summer. I hope you root for my Zilah and her adventures with Daniel. I wasn't easy on her, but then she wouldn't expect it. She would just go forward with quiet strength and maybe give us her summer smile.

Iris Johansen

1

The young woman in the photograph was smiling. It was a summer smile, warm and wise yet brimming with the promise of richness and beauty still to come.

She was dressed in jeans and a plaid cotton western shirt and was sitting on the back of a beautiful palomino horse. Her green eyes held the serenity and gravity of a much older woman, but her lips were slightly parted and her face lit with such warmth and eagerness that it caused Daniel's hand to tighten involuntarily on the snapshot. "Very pretty." He forced his voice to sound casual. "What did you say her name was?"

"Zilah Dabala." Clancy Donahue leaned back, his ice blue eyes narrowed on the man in the executive chair behind the desk. "You met her mother two years ago when I took you to that party at Karim's. She's in charge of the housekeeping for all of his houses."

"Yes, I remember her," Daniel murmured, still gazing absently at the photograph.

Clancy had known he would. He would wager Daniel Seifert could recall every person and incident that had crossed his path in the last ten years. It was one of the abilities that had made him invaluable as Clancy's first lieutenant in Sedikhan's security service for over two years. That, along with a lethal deadliness that was honed to razor sharpness, had made him a weapon more potent than any in Clancy's extensive arsenal. "Yasmin is a very fine woman and terribly worried about Zilah."

"She doesn't look like her mother." As Daniel recalled, Yasmin was an attractive woman in her late forties with an olive complexion and dark hair and eyes. The woman in the picture had a skin tone that appeared to be pale gold rather than olive. Her wideset eyes were slightly uptilted at the corners and were a beautiful shade of clear, pale green. Her hair wasn't dark but a light tan, sunstreaked with gold, and tumbled down her back in a straight shining curtain.

"Her mother is a native of Sedikhan," Clancy said. "Zilah's only half Sedikhanese. But she's intimately linked to those in power

through her association with David Bradford."

"Bradford?" Daniel tore his gaze from the
photograph to glance up swiftly. "What the
devil does Bradford have to do with this?"

"Zilah and he go back a long way." Clancy
paused. "You might say she's something of
a protégée of David's."

"Really?" Daniel's lips twisted in a cynical
smile. "And I heard he was so much in love
with that copper-haired wife of his." He
studied the photograph appraisingly. "However, Zilah is certainly lovely enough to be
any man's prize 'protégée.' A little young
for Bradford though, isn't she?"

"She's twenty-one and she's not —"
Clancy broke off. "I'm not at liberty to
discuss Zilah's relationship with David."

Daniel shrugged. "I wouldn't think of pry-
ing into the man's personal life. It's nothing
to me if he keeps a hundred women on the
side." He tossed the photograph onto the
desk in front of him and resolutely kept his
eyes away from it. Why the hell was he feeling this helpless fascination with the girl in
the photograph? It didn't make any sense at
all. She was lovely, but the Khadim who had
occupied his bed the night before was far
more beautiful. Lord, he had even felt a
surge of sheer possessive rage when Clancy

9

had identified her as Bradford's mistress.

He leaned back in his chair and drew up one knee to rest against the desk. "I can see how her closeness to Bradford might be a weapon in the terrorists' hands." He had never met David Bradford, but Daniel was well aware that the man was regarded with deep affection by both Sheikh Alex Ben Raschid, who was the reigning monarch of Sedikhan, and his wife Sabrina. Even old Karim Ben Raschid, the former ruler, was tremendously fond of him. "Yes, if Bradford chose to exert a little muscle on behalf of his *chère amie,* there's no doubt he would have the ear to the throne."

Clancy nodded grimly. "You're damn right he would. David would be just as upset as Yasmin if he knew about the hijacking. That's why Alex wants this mess cleaned up before David hears about it."

Daniel lifted a brow. "He doesn't know about it yet?"

"He's in New York at the moment with his wife, Billie. She had to fly to the U.S. to sign a contract for a song she's written."

"And, of course, Alex doesn't want his old friend to have his domestic bliss shattered by this very inconvenient hijacking," Daniel said caustically.

Clancy's brow knotted in a frown. "Let's

10

just say he doesn't want David to be made unhappy by this matter. And why the hell are you harping on David's association with Zilah, anyway? You're not exactly a puritan, Daniel."

"I'm not harping. I just —" Daniel broke off. He was harping and he knew it. How could he explain his anger at the idea of Bradford making love to the woman in that photograph when he didn't understand it himself? "You're right. I sure as hell haven't the right to cast the first stone." He clasped his hands around his knee. "Okay, fill me in. So far you've told me only that four terrorists have hijacked a Sedikhan Oil Company plane and are holding Zilah Dabala and the pilot hostage to force Ben Raschid to release two of their group from a Sedikhan prison. I gather you wouldn't be here unless you wanted my help. What's the scenario?" A slight smile touched his lips. "I admit to being curious about why you think I'd be interested in the job after my two years in official retirement."

Clancy scowled. "Alex was overgenerous, as usual. How does he expect me to run an efficient security system if he makes my best man rich enough to quit the business?"

"You could have suggested that he not give me those oil wells," Daniel said with a

11

grin. "Your opinion carries a good deal of weight with Alex."

"After you saved Sabrina and her son when that nut tried to shoot them?" Clancy asked sourly. "I'm just surprised he didn't give you a seat on the board of Sedikhan Oil as well."

"He offered to do that, but I told him I'd just as soon the company stayed solvent." Daniel's eyes were twinkling. "I'm no businessman."

"No, your talents lie in other directions," Clancy agreed. "And so does your experience. That's why I'm here. I would have handled the matter myself but the situation has become a little touchy."

"Touchy?"

"As in complicated." Clancy's lips tightened. "All right, here's the way it's shaping up." He leaned forward in the cane chair and his words fired out with machine-gun rapidity. "The terrorists are headed by one Ali Hassan, who is the brother of one of the prisoners being held in Marasef. We think the group has been waiting for this chance for a long time. They've done their homework if they've linked David with Zilah. She's been in the United States for a number of years and is presently attending Texas A&M University." For a moment there was a flicker of impersonal admiration in his expression. "They're not stupid. They've picked their target very carefully. The security around Alex, his family and his friends is almost impregnable. Zilah, on the other hand, is on the outer fringe of that circle and yet is close to one of its most important members. They must have been watching for an opportunity, and when Karim arranged for the company plane to fly Zilah home to Sedikhan, they pounced. They managed to substitute one of their own men for the copilot, and when they were airborne out of Houston, he made his move. That was yesterday morning. They landed in the Madrona Desert and were met by the other three terrorists."

"The Madrona Desert?" Daniel's eyes narrowed. "The Madrona begins only a few miles from here. They landed in Sedikhan territory?"

"I told you they weren't stupid. They landed across the border in Said Ababa. They knew that government has been hostile to Alex's regime and would conveniently ignore their presence there." He paused. "And the Sedikhan province closest to their location is this one, and it's ruled by your old friend, Philip El Kabbar. Are you beginning to get the picture?"

13

"It's starting to come into focus," Daniel said. "Philip is one of the most powerful sheikhs in Sedikhan: Alex never enters this province without Philip's express consent. Since Philip is almost as autocratic as Alex, it might take days before that consent is given." His hands dropped from his knee and he straightened slowly in his chair. "You're right, this group of terrorists must be pretty damn sharp."

"But we have one ace in the hole." Clancy's gaze dropped significantly to the gold ring on Daniel's left hand with its exotically beautiful design of a rose in full bloom pierced by a sword. "You saved El Kabbar's life several years ago, and since you retired you've occupied this house only a stone's throw from his own. You've become good friends with him." A slight smile tugged at his lips. "Hell, I've even seen newspaper pictures of the two of you jetsetting together in Paris and Monte Carlo. Quite a change for a man of your background, Daniel. Are you enjoying your newly acquired wealth?"

"It's all right, I suppose. It has its moments." Daniel's gaze sharpened. "You want me to intercede with Philip for you?"

"No," Clancy said calmly. "I want you to go into Said Ababa alone and bring out the girl. And I want you to do it in such a way

14

that Hassan and his men will follow you back into Sedikhan."

For a moment Daniel stared at him in stunned disbelief. Then he started to laugh. "Good God, I suppose I should be flattered. Who do you think I am, anyway? Superman?"

"You're a damn good agent and you've pulled off stunts as difficult as this before." Clancy tilted his head objectively. "If anyone can do it, you can. We don't have a hell of a lot of choice. You're the only man El Kabbar would tolerate violating his territorial border." Clancy's voice became grim. "There's no possibility that Alex will release those prisoners. That terrorist group planted a bomb on a schoolbus, and it seriously injured several children when it went off. Alex wants those bastards, and if El Kabbar is angered by them and what they're doing in his province, they'll never reach Marasef."

"I'm relieved that you don't want me to wipe all four of them out at one swoop," Daniel said caustically. "Just grab the woman, cross fifty miles of desert and another five through the hills. Then, *if* we make it to the border, I'm to keep Philip from carving up any possible pursuers and serve them to Alex myself on a silver platter. Nothing to it."

"I've always liked a man with confidence," Clancy said with a bland smile. "I take it you're accepting the assignment?"

"Why is it necessary to go in alone?"

"We've told them we don't deal until we verify that Zilah is alive and well. The terrorists have agreed to let a man come into the plane for that purpose, but only one man. They've also agreed to release the pilot and deliver him to the mosque in Said Ababa as a gesture of good faith. The delivery will take place at two o'clock tomorrow afternoon. They'll probably delegate two men to take the pilot to the mosque, which is about thirty miles from the plane." Clancy paused. "That will leave only two men to guard Zilah. I suggest if you're going to make a move, that would be the ideal time. We'll tell them you'll be there to check on Zilah at two-fifteen." Clancy stood up. "I have a few gadgets in my helicopter that might interest you. I'll go get them."

Daniel's lips curved in grim amusement. He was very familiar with Clancy's arsenal of gadgets. He had no doubt that these particular items would prove most lethal as well as interesting.

"When will you be ready to leave?" Clancy

had paused at the door. "I imagine you'll want some time to reconnoiter the area."

"What makes you think you've convinced me to go?" Daniel drawled. "I'm not a complete madman, Clancy."

Clancy shook his dark head. The rays of the late afternoon sun streaming into the study revealed the flecks of silver in its rich thickness. The smile on his craggy face was weary and faintly rueful. "Any man in our line of work has to be a little mad. You've lived on the edge of danger most of your life, Daniel. Don't tell me you're not bored out of your skull with the tame, easy life. Hell, I don't have to *convince* you to take the job. All I have to do is offer it to you." He turned away. "I'll be back in ten minutes."

Daniel gazed bemusedly at the closed door for a moment. Then he began to chuckle. Damn, there was no one like Clancy. He had missed him in the last two years. Daniel's glance drifted restlessly around the luxurious study, with its rich Oriental carpet and the art objects that were as exquisite as the room itself. All very tasteful and civilized and — He suddenly pushed back his chair with leashed violence and stood up. And *boring,* dammit. So godawful boring that he was barely able to restrain

17

the violence that his restlessness engendered. Clancy knew him very well. He wasn't destined to be a playboy. It had been amusing for all of three months before pleasure had palled and boredom had reared its head. No wonder Clancy had been so confident that he would jump at this impossibly difficult mission.

He glanced down at the girl in the photograph, and a reckless smile curved his lips. One finger reached out and caressingly touched the mouth of the girl. A summer smile. Why not admit that it wasn't only the danger that was the attraction but the idea of bedding Bradford's lovely protégée? It had to be lust that he was feeling. Anything else was too absurd to accept. That first odd impression of finding something that had been lost was pure imagination. Yes, it had to be lust.

Hell, he was beginning to look with genuine anticipation on the coming mission, he thought with a grin. Clancy Donahue was probably right. He must be a little mad. The smile still lingered as he strode briskly across the room and out the study door to help Clancy bring in his amusing little "gadgets."

"You will tell him that we have treated you

like a delicate flower." Ali Hassan dropped down into the seat beside Zilah, a smile of sleek satisfaction on his narrow, catlike face. "That you have been fed and allowed to sleep. We have not beaten you or used you sexually. You will tell him these things when he asks. You understand?"

"I will tell him." Zilah leaned her head back wearily against the cushioned headrest of her seat. She touched her cut lower lip gingerly. "However, I don't think he'll believe me when he sees this little memento."

"You should not have tried to snatch the gun from Hakim." Hassan shrugged. "It was a stupid move. We have no wish to harm you. You are too valuable to us."

"You're insane to believe that Sheikh Ben Raschid will give you what you want. I'm nothing to him." Her hands tightened on the padded arms of the seat. "In the end he'll refuse your demands."

Hassan's smile faded. "I hope for your sake he is not so foolish. Your treatment will change radically at that point." His hand dropped to rest with insulting intimacy on her jean-clad thigh. "You are a very beautiful woman, Zilah Dabala. My friends and I would enjoy using you." He felt the muscles of her thigh tense beneath his hand, and there was another flicker of satisfaction in his dark eyes. "Did you know I was a student at the university at Marasef eight years ago?"

Zilah felt the breath leave her body; panic rose within her. She knew what was coming. It was there in the expression of feline satisfaction on his face. She mustn't give in to the panic. She *wouldn't* give in to it. She was strong. David had made her strong. "How could I know that?" She lifted her chin defiantly. "I haven't noticed any measurable degree of educated intelligence in your actions so far. I'm surprised that they let you into any university."

His fingers tightened on her thigh with a sudden force that brought an involuntary cry of pain from her. "So proud," he sneered. "Have you forgotten the House of the Yellow Door so quickly?"

"I *have* forgotten it," Zilah said quietly. "It doesn't exist for me any longer."

"If Bradford fails to persuade Ben Raschid that we are serious, we will remind you. Be sure of it." Hassan's hand relaxed and fell away from her thigh. He stood up. "You might shed a few frightened tears for this Daniel Seifert to report back to Bradford. It wouldn't hurt." He turned away and made a sign to his cohort, who was lounging in a seat at the front of the plane, a machine-gun lying carelessly in the crook of his arm. "Seifert should be here in five minutes. We will meet him outside and conduct a routine search. I doubt if Ben Raschid would be foolish enough to send one man against us, but Hakim and I will make sure."

He threw open the heavy metal door and went down the steps of the Learjet. Zilah saw that he said something over his shoulder to Hakim, who was following close behind him, and then laughed. She leaned back in her seat and closed her eyes. Animals. They were animals, and she mustn't let Hassan's words touch her.

It was so hot in the cabin that she could scarcely breathe. Perspiration was running down her back, causing her short-sleeved white shirt to cling to her like a second skin. She opened her eyes and stared numbly out the window at the desolate wasteland of sand. Nothing but dunes and sky as far as the eye could see, and the heat was rising from those dunes in shimmering waves.

She wouldn't be afraid. There must be some way she could escape Hassan and his men if she could rid herself of this debilitating fear. The last twenty-four hours had been a nightmare of terror. Yet she couldn't let them use her like this. David

21

had done so much for her; she couldn't allow herself to be turned into a weapon against him.

The throbbing chug of a motor caused her to straighten swiftly and lean closer to the window. A jeep had halted a good fifty yards from the plane and the driver lithely swung to the ground. His hands rose quickly above his head. "Daniel Seifert," he called.

He should have looked cowed and intimidated in that position, but there was nothing in the least tame about the man who was standing with his legs astride beside the open jeep. He was a giant of a man, at least six foot five or perhaps taller, and dressed in khaki trousers that outlined the powerful muscles of his thighs and calves. His khaki shirt seemed barely able to contain the sleek biceps of those massive arms. Auburn hair blazed in the sunlight and a closely trimmed mustache and beard were of the same fiery hue as his hair. He was a wild, barbaric figure and reminded her vaguely of a painting she'd once seen of a fierce Viking warrior.

Hassan and Hakim must have been equally impressed by the air of restrained menace that Seifert exuded because their attitude was distinctly wary as they approached him. They ordered him to lean

22

against the hood of the jeep. The search wasn't the routine one Hassan had planned. It was very thorough but yielded nothing more lethal than a fingernail clipper. Then they were striding toward the plane, the red-haired giant a few paces ahead, apparently ignoring the machine-gun Hakim was pointing at the small of his back.

"Relax," Hassan snapped at Hakim as they entered the passenger compartment of the plane. "You saw that there was no sign of a weapon. It appears Ben Raschid is being sensible for a change." He gestured to Zilah in her seat at the back of the plane. "There she is, Seifert. You can see that she's alive and unharmed."

"I want to talk to her," Daniel said. "Alone."

"That's not necessary," Hassan said sharply. "She will tell you we have not misused her."

"Then let her tell me," Daniel said. "Alone. I have instructions to make sure you've done her no harm before we deal. I hardly think she'd be willing to spill any beans while you stand there with a gun pointed at her head."

Hassan hesitated a moment before he shrugged. "Go ahead. We will stay by the door. You will be out of earshot back there if you lower your voice. You have five minutes."

Daniel Seifert looked even bigger in the confines of the cabin than he had by the jeep as he strode down the aisle toward her. He sat down in the seat facing her, his gaze searching her face. "My name is Daniel Seifert. Have they hurt you?"

"Not really. It doesn't matter." She moistened her lips nervously. "You have to tell Sheikh Ben Raschid not to give in to them. I'll get out of this by myself."

"Oh, will you?" Daniel asked sardonically. "That might be a little difficult considering the circumstances."

"I told you. I'll handle it. I owe too many debts already. I can't add a burden like this to them."

He was silent for a long moment, studying her intently. "You mean it."

"Of course I mean it. I don't say things I don't mean," she said, impatient. "Now, will you tell David and the sheikh I'm fine and that I'll find a way out of this mess myself?"

He shook his head. "We'll talk about it later," he said. Zilah Dabala looked more tired and more finely drawn than she had in the photograph, but the clear green eyes meeting his were steady and unafraid. There was no summer smile, however. Her lips

24

were taut with the effort she was making to keep them from trembling. Strange that he could miss a smile he'd never really seen outside of a photograph. Suddenly his gaze sharpened as he realized that a cut marred the softness of her lower lip. His expression hardened into a fierceness that startled her. "Who struck you? I thought you said you hadn't been hurt."

Her fingers flew automatically to the cut on her lip. "Hassan. Stupidly, I tried to grab a gun from Hakim. I won't do anything so impulsive again." She deliberately dropped her hand away. "See, it's only a little cut. It doesn't hurt. And, anyway, it doesn't matter."

"It matters." His tone was granite-harsh. His finger rose to brush her lower lip with a gossamer touch.

Zilah felt a sudden sensation that was like nothing she had ever experienced before. It must be pain, she thought in bewilderment. But somehow it didn't feel like pain. It was more like a hot tingle of pleasure. Daniel Seifert's navy blue eyes were holding her own with mesmerizing power.

"It matters very much." His voice had softened to dark richness. Then he shifted so that his bulk was between her and the men in the front of the plane. "I'll take care of Hassan soon. It will be a pleasure I'll look forward to." His voice was a mere whisper. "We haven't much time. Be ready."

Zilah's brow knotted in puzzlement. "Ready for what?"

"There will be intense pain." Daniel was speaking rapidly, his eyes on her face. "I'm sorry, but I couldn't think of any other way. I knew I'd be searched, so I couldn't bring anything along to protect you. Will you trust me?"

"You're going to —"

"Trust me," he said again. "I won't let anything happen to you. Just hold on to me until hell freezes over. You won't be sorry."

She met his worried gaze. Gentleness, regret, and some other emotion she couldn't define were conflicting in that brutally powerful face. She smiled. "I'll hold on to you until hell freezes over. I promise." He returned her smile. How odd that warm gentle smile looked in the rough-hewn boldness of his warrior face.

"Good. I'll damn well remind you of that promise if you forget. We're in this together, Zilah."

She nodded. "Toge —" The word was shattered as an explosion rocked the plane. "What!"

Within seconds of each other there was a

chain of explosions that appeared to encircle the plane. After that the action was so lightning-fast that she perceived it only as a blur.

Daniel reached into his back pocket and brought out a pristine white handkerchief. "Cover your nose and mouth and keep your eyes closed. Try to hold your breath."

Then he tore off his left ear!

A false ear, she realized almost immediately as he balled it up in his palm.

The explosions were still going on outside the plane. Hassan was shouting something to the other man, who was peering through the window to try to sight their attackers.

Confusion became sheer madness as Daniel threw the object in his hand into their midst. Cerise smoke suddenly filled the plane.

Zilah's mouth was agape with astonishment. The spell was broken as Daniel gave her an exasperated glance. "Dammit, cover your face!"

She heard a scream of agony from Hakim somewhere in that thick red mist ahead. She quickly covered her mouth and nose with the handkerchief.

"Come on." Daniel was on his feet. "Grab on to my belt. I may have to have my hands free."

She heard another scream. Hassan?

She closed her eyes as they entered the thick mist by the door but not before she caught a shadowy glimpse of Hassan. He was doubled over, his hands over his eyes, and clutching desperately at his face. His rifle was on the floor beside him.

Pain struck her!

Her face was a fiery agony. The cloth of the handkerchief was offering almost no protection against the heavy fumes by the door. She halted, stunned by the sheer intensity of the pain. She heard a muttered imprecation from Daniel, and then his arm was around her, pushing her through the door, down the stairs, and out into the sunlight. The desert heat enveloped her, suffocating her. They were running toward the jeep, she realized. Another round of explosions was going off, shaking the earth beneath her feet and causing puffs of fire and smoke to appear like lethal blossoms on the starkness of the dunes.

Daniel's hands were encircling her waist, lifting, almost throwing her into the jeep. He jumped into the driver's seat and put the jeep into gear. The windshield in front of them exploded in a cobweb of splinters with a neat hole in the center. A bullet hole! She glanced back to see Hassan a few yards from the plane aiming again with the rifle. Hakim was stumbling down the steps of the plane, still reeling with pain.

"Get down!" Daniel's roar was so harsh, she obeyed instantly. "Dammit, I was hoping the gas would give us a few more minutes." His foot jammed down on the accelerator and the jeep leaped forward. Another bullet whistled past her head and ricocheted off the frame of the windshield. Daniel began to zigzag across the sands. Other shots followed, hitting somewhere in the rear of the jeep. Daniel was fumbling underneath the seat and bringing out a small black metal box.

"What's that?" Zilah had to shout to be heard over the roar of the motor and the hail of bullets.

"I was going to wait until we were farther away, but I think we need the distraction more than the distance." Daniel pressed the red button on the box.

The earth heaved as an explosion four times as strong as the previous ones rocked the desert. She glanced back over her shoulder to see that the Learjet was now nothing but a blazing inferno. "You blew up the plane!"

"I told you we needed a distraction." He looked back over his shoulder. Hakim, who had been close to the plane, had been knocked off his feet and was crawling with desperate swiftness away from the flaming wreckage. Another rifle shot sounded. "Hassan doesn't appear to have been stopped, but I think we're out of range now."

"You blew up the plane," she repeated, dazed.

"Ben Raschid wants them," Daniel said calmly. "I didn't want to chance them turning chicken and flying out of here. I also wanted to make them mad enough to come after us across the border."

"You *planned* for them to follow us?"

"You're damn right." His grin took on a touch of ferocity as he shot a sideways glance at her. His gaze lingered on her swollen lip. "I've decided that I want them too."

She was wiping her streaming eyes with the handkerchief. "Well, I don't think there's any question you succeeded in making them mad enough. When the other two men return with the jeep, they'll probably be hot on our trail."

"Probably. But by that time we'll be out of this desert and halfway through the hills. You'll be across the border and safe at my friend's compound before they reach Sedikhan." His lips tightened grimly. "And then I'll go on a little hunting trip."

A shiver ran through her. The ferocity was no longer a touch but glittering sharp as a dagger in his face. Daniel Seifert was obviously a very dangerous man. For an instant she felt almost sorry for Hassan and his men. Then she realized just how ridiculous that thought was. He was only one man, for heaven's sake. Clearly an extraordinary man, judging from his actions in the past half hour, but not invulnerable. "No," she said quietly. "I've caused enough trouble. I don't want you to put yourself in any more danger because of me."

"My choice," he said tersely. "You don't have anything to say about it. I want them."

"I *do* have something to say about it." Her green eyes were suddenly sparking. "I'm very grateful for your help, but I won't accept any more from you. I'll handle everything from now on."

"We'll see about that," Daniel muttered.

The glance she threw at him was exasperated. She felt as if she were beating her head against a stone wall. "I mean it, you know."

He patted her knee affectionately. "I know you do." His smile was so warm and gentle, she could almost forget the harshness that had been there before. "You seem to think you can handle the whole damn world."

She lifted her chin. "I can."

31

He chuckled, his dark blue eyes twinkling. "Maybe you can at that. It will be fun to stick around and at least see you try."

She frowned. "How did you do it?"

His brow lifted inquiringly.

"My rescue. It was quite spectacular." She shook her head in wonder. "Almost unbelievable."

"I'm very good," he said with a roguish grin. "I've been known to boggle the mind on occasion."

"You've certainly succeeded in boggling mine. It was like something out of a James Bond movie."

"The fireworks were a little theatrical, I admit. I have a tendency to be somewhat flamboyant, but it doesn't make me any less effective. Clancy Donahue is also very fond of gadgets and indulges me."

"You're one of Clancy's agents?"

His expression hardened. "I'd forgotten how familiar you are with Bradford and his friends. I was one of Clancy's lieutenants, but I'm retired now. This is in the nature of a special mission." His grim expression dissolved into a reckless grin. "He offered me something I couldn't refuse."

"It must have been very valuable to cause you to risk your life."

"I think it may prove to be priceless." His

gaze held her own for a long moment, and she experienced that same bewildering sensation as when he had touched her lip on the plane. But he wasn't touching her now, she thought. Only with his eyes and that smile that caused an almost physical rapport. She hurriedly looked away. "You didn't answer me. How did you do it?"

He shrugged. "I spent most of the night planting those charges and setting the timers. The only dicey one was on the fuselage of the plane. If Hassan's outside guard had been on the ball, he would have spotted me. There was no ground cover."

"Was that a tear gas bomb you exploded on the plane?"

He shook his head. "It was one of Clancy's chemical specials, created to affect the sinuses and the respiratory tract. It's far more sophisticated than tear gas, as well as much more painful. One good whiff and it almost completely incapacitates a man." His eyes darkened with concern. "Are you all right?"

She nodded. "My chest aches and I can't seem to stop crying. Otherwise I'm fine." She frowned. "But how did you manage to stand it with nothing to cover your face?"

"Nose plugs and contact lenses." He grimaced. "Together with that damned false ear I felt like the bionic man from the television series."

"Oh, yes, the false ear." She shook her head and chuckled. "I nearly fell over when you tore your left ear off. It looked so real."

"Nothing but the best for Clancy. He *did* give me a choice of which appendage I wanted to duplicate for the bomb. But there were only two choices, and the other appendage I refused to destroy even in effigy." He glanced casually at the gauges on the panel in front of him and his smile disappeared. He uttered a brief but violent curse.

"What's wrong?"

"The gas, dammit. The gauge is dropping like a stone. One of the bullets must have hit the gas tank."

Her eyes widened apprehensively. "We're almost out of gas?"

He nodded. "And we're still a good ten miles from the beginning of the foothills. We'll be lucky if the jeep makes it another eight or nine miles. We'll still have to hike a mile or two in the desert."

"Is that all?" Zilah breathed a sigh of relief. "I thought we were going to be stranded out here for Hassan and his men to find."

"It's bad enough. It means that we'll have

only a short head start on Hassan and may have to play hide-and-seek in those hills tonight. We'll have to stay off the main paths. We'll be lucky if we get to the border by tomorrow morning."

She shrugged. "It doesn't matter when we get there, just so we do. A night in the hills won't be so terrible."

"You can handle it?" he asked mockingly.

"I can handle anything," she said in a grave tone of voice. "I've had an excellent teacher."

His lips tightened. "Bradford?"

She nodded. "David taught me practically everything I know." Her voice softened. "He's a wonderful, wonderful man."

"I'm sure he enjoys enormously the manner in which you express your gratitude," Daniel said harshly. "But I'll wager there are still a few lessons you could learn."

She stared at him, clearly puzzled. "I don't know what you mean."

His boot suddenly jammed on the accelerator with a force that caused the jeep to buck. Then, realizing that the impulsive action had wasted precious gas, he cursed beneath his breath. "You will." His gaze was fixed on the hills wavering in the distance like a cool, verdant mirage. "I assure you that I have every intention that you understand me very well."

They were some nine miles closer to those hills when the jeep sputtered, choked, and then came to a halt.

"Out," Daniel ordered tersely, swinging his long legs over the side of the jeep.

Zilah was already scrambling from her seat as he spoke. The sand was hot beneath the rubber soles of her tennis shoes. It would probably get hotter, she thought grimly. She had better get accustomed to it. She joined Daniel at the back of the jeep, where he was raising a false bottom panel on the floor before the rear seats.

He quickly pulled out an army-green backpack, a canteen, and a lethally efficient-looking rifle complete with carrying strap. He thrust the gun at her. "Hold on to this for a minute, will you?"

She accepted the rifle with a faint sensation of unreality. It looked like an army issue machine-gun of some sort. Who would have believed a few days ago at peaceful Texas A&M that she would be here in the desert holding a rifle with which only a man like Daniel Seifert would be comfortable? She watched bemusedly as Daniel extracted the noseplugs and contact lenses he was wearing and threw them carelessly on the backseat. Then he was strapping on the backpack with swift, economical movements. He took the rifle, slung it over his shoulder, and reached for the canteen.

"Let me carry the rifle," Zilah said quietly. "It makes no sense for you to be burdened with all of the equipment. I want to do my share."

He shook his head. "We have to move fast. I want to be halfway up that first hill in twenty minutes — tops!" His lips tightened. "It may be all the time we have." He gave her the canteen. "Hang on to this. The rest of this stuff is no problem for me." He grinned. "In case you haven't noticed, I'm as big as a house. It comes in handy once in a while." He took her hand. "Come on, hike!"

She slung the canteen over her shoulder and fell into step with him. His clasp on her hand was warmly comforting, yet she was still conscious of that bewildering tingling of awareness. She had the odd feeling that a part of her was being absorbed by his grasp. It made her vaguely uneasy and she instinctively tried to pull away. He released her at once and she immediately felt a little foolish.

His gaze flew down to her face. "You're frowning," he noticed. "Are you frightened?"

"Yes," she said honestly. "I'm scared to death. I have been ever since you tore off that ridiculous false ear and exploded the gas." She looked directly at him. "But you needn't worry about me falling apart. I know you have enough problems without having a hysterical woman on your hands. Just tell me what to do and I'll do it."

His brow rose quizzically. "Just like that? No indignant protests? No women's lib? No ranting about your right to have a say in all this?"

"I'm not a fool," she said. "This type of action is obviously your métier, not mine. When you're with an expert, you get out of his way and let him do his job." Her lips curved in an ironic smile. "I'll help in any way I can, but I'm afraid that blowing up airplanes wasn't in my college curriculum."

"I'd never know it. You're a very cool lady when the chips are down." His expression softened. "Try not to worry too much. I'm not saying this is going to be easy, but I have no intention of letting Hassan get hold of you again. I don't like to lose. I make a habit of avoiding it at all costs."

"I hope this isn't the exception that proves the rule," she said, trying to smile.

"It won't be." His eyes narrowed intently on her face. "I have a very special reason for wanting to win this time. Trust me."

"Until hell freezes over?"

"It worked out pretty well the last time, didn't it?" He glanced away. "We'd better put on more speed. There's no place out here in the open to dig in if we don't have as much time as I've been calculating."

"All right." She increased her pace to match his. She did trust him, she realized with a little ripple of shock. She trusted not only his proficiency in his very dangerous profession but the man himself. She was usually on edge when she was around strange men, particularly dynamic, virile men. Yet, oddly, this wasn't the case with Daniel Seifert. In spite of the bewildering physical responses he was inspiring within her, she felt as if there were a bond between them that had been woven by years, not mere minutes.

Well, she had no time now to analyze that unusual rapport. Perhaps it was merely due to the crisis situation they shared. She shook her head. She was getting as bad as all those psychiatrists about dissecting her own reactions and responses. She had to concentrate on keeping up with Daniel's constantly lengthening stride. She cast an anxious glance over her shoulder. No sign of Hassan. However, that didn't mean he wouldn't appear on the horizon at any minute. Her pace automatically quickened at the thought, and her gaze fixed determinedly on the hills just ahead.

2

"Here they come," Daniel murmured. He shaded his eyes with his hand to watch the approaching jeep kick up clouds of sand on the desert floor far below the summit of the hill on which they were standing. "They're really gunning it. They must have found our abandoned jeep and think they have us."

"And do they?" Zilah asked with a worried frown. "They're so close. They'll be here within ten minutes, won't they?"

"Just about." He turned and took her elbow. She felt that same mysterious tingling surge through her and had to restrain herself from jerking her arm away. What on earth was happening to her? This touch wasn't even like the other time. It was almost totally impersonal. "But we won't be here. We're not following the road. We're heading through the trees and over that next hill. Then we'll circle and rejoin the road at the border."

"You seem to know this area very well."

"Philip and I have done some hunting in these hills."

"Philip?"

"Philip El Kabbar. He's an old friend of mine." He shot her a glance. "You've never heard of him?"

She shook her head. "I've spent the last seven years on a ranch in Texas. Should I be familiar with the name?"

"He's probably the most powerful sheikh in Sedikhan other than Ben Raschid." He was propelling her down from the summit on which they had been standing, hurrying from the path into the dense shrubbery that lined it. "That long? That must have been a trifle inconvenient for Bradford."

"Inconvenient?" she asked, puzzled. "It was David's parents' ranch, but I tried not to be a burden to them. Once I learned to ride I could help around the ranch."

"You've been stashed at David Bradford's disposal since you were fourteen?" Daniel's tone was caustic. "My Lord, you started young."

"I don't know what you mea . . ." Her eyes widened. "You think David is my lover?"

He held a branch until she had passed and then let it snap back behind them. "It's none of my affair." Then he shot her a glance that shocked her with its ferocity. "The hell it's not. It *is* my business. I've been trying to convince myself since I saw a damned photograph of you that you're just like any other woman. No more and no less. But I've never lied to myself and I don't intend to start now. You *are* my concern." His face was flint hard. "I walked down the aisle of that plane on which you were held just a few hours ago and I knew you were going to belong to me. Get used to the idea. I don't know what the hell has happened to me, but I do know that." He shoved another branch roughly aside and pushed her ahead of him. "You can tell David Bradford he'll just have to be satisfied with his wife. You're no longer available."

"He couldn't be more satisfied with Billie," she said dazedly. "And I'm not going to belong to you. We're complete strangers. This is insane. We've just met. There are four half-crazy terrorists snapping at our heels and you're propositioning me?"

"Propositioning, hell! I'm telling you." He was pushing her steadily forward, the harshness of his voice at strange variance with the exquisite care he was exhibiting in protecting her from the branches and roughness of the bushes and trees surrounding them. "Do you think I don't know how I

43

sound? I'm fully aware I'm not being rational, that I'm reacting like some kind of thick-headed neanderthal. I can't help myself, dammit." He glared at her accusingly. "And I don't like not being in control. It annoys the hell out of me."

"You're acting as if it's my fault you're having this temporary aberration," she said incredulously. "I didn't have anything to do with it."

"I know that, too." He scowled moodily. "My problem is that I'm not at all sure it *is* temporary."

She laughed shakily. "It has to be."

"Does it?" His lips twisted. "We'll just have to see. It's too soon to tell. Temporary or not, you're still mine. And I'll tell Bradford so if you're shy about it." His grin was a savage slash in the blaze of his bearded face. "I'd enjoy telling him."

"I don't belong to anyone. Not to you, and certainly not to David." She was trembling, she realized with amazement. For the first time in her adult life a man had effortlessly pierced the wall she had built around her emotions. He had scarcely touched her in the past hours except with his words. Yet she was acutely aware of his very presence. Her heart was pounding, her mouth was dry, and she felt as if she had a fever. His fingers on her arm were as impersonal as his words were possessive, but her flesh was so sensitive that she could feel the drumming of his heart through the pads of his fingertips. How could she feel like this when she had to force herself to bear even the most casual touch of any other man? She tried to jerk her arm away, but her resistance was instantly quelled by a tightening of those fingers. "Let me go."

"No, you need me." He didn't even look at her as he increased his pace. "You need me now and you're going to need me even more later. But not in the same way, I assure you. I'll fill every damn need you have. Bradford is out of your life."

She moistened her lips. "David will never be out of my life. You don't understand. David is my friend. I'm not his mistress." She shook her head. "The idea is almost laughable. He's completely in love with his wife, Billie."

"I notice you're not mentioning your own feelings in the matter." Daniel's lips twisted. "You're obviously just as mad about him as he is about his wife. All he'd have to do is snap his fingers and you'd jump into his bed."

Her gaze was steady and perfectly candid. "I'd give the last drop of blood in my veins if David Bradford wanted or needed it." She shrugged. "As for my body, there's no question he could have it. It wouldn't matter at all."

"The hell it wouldn't!" Daniel's voice was so violent that it startled her. "It would matter to me." He drew a deep breath, and when he spoke again it was through clenched teeth. "I think you better shut up. At the moment I'm feeling pretty wild. I might just show you how much it could matter to you as well. That would be slightly unwise, as Hassan would probably appear on the scene and shoot my ass off."

"That would be a little inconvenient." She tried to smile. "As well as being totally useless. There's no way you can convince me that the sexual act is more than a simple animalistic coupling."

"No? You're speaking like a frustrated, antiquated virgin. If we weren't in the wrong place at the wrong time to —" He broke off as he saw the strange wounded look in her eyes. "What the hell's wrong with you? You're looking at me as if I'd stabbed you."

"Am I?" Her voice was shaky in spite of her efforts to steady it. "How stupid of me." She began to walk faster. "I'm not a virgin, you know. I haven't been for a long time. You were right, I started very young." She was speaking quickly, almost feverishly. "But not with David Bradford. Never with David."

He suddenly halted in the path and swung her around to face him. "Will you shut up and let me look at you, dammit." His gaze raked her tense face, and he began to curse with low and intense sincerity. "I've hurt you. What the hell did I say that hurt you so much?"

"Nothing." She tried to loosen his hold. "I told you I was being stupid. Let's get going. We've got to keep moving, haven't we?"

"Yes," he said. His hands were kneading her shoulders absently as he stared into her face. "But I'm not going on until you tell me why you're hurting." His eyes narrowed thoughtfully. "Was it that crack I made about virgins? I've heard Sedikhan society is pretty straightlaced." He gave her a little shake. "I don't give a damn how young you were when you had your first man." His lips twisted in a rueful grin. "I'd make a bet that I was probably younger than you when I had my first woman. I don't have any right to ask something of you that I can't give in return." His smile deepened and took on a gentleness that caused her heart to jerk crazily and then melt like the snows of spring. "I didn't mean to hurt you. I'm a

47

rough man and I've lived a rough life but you don't have to be afraid of me. I'll never hurt you intentionally." His finger touched the outer edge of her lower lip. "And I'll never let anyone else hurt you. Do you believe me?"

His touch was so light; how could it have such powerful sensuality? She felt every brush of his fingertip, not only on her lips but in her wrists, the pit of her stomach, and the soles of her feet. She was tingling all over and he wasn't even trying to arouse her in a sensual way. She was conscious of the scent of him surrounding her. The clean smell of soap, the musky odor of sweat and man. She suddenly wanted to reach up and touch the dark, flaming softness of his beard and trace the well-defined curve of his lip as he was touching hers. She actually wanted to *touch* him, she realized with a sense of shock.

She lowered her eyes hurriedly to the center of his chest, but it did little to alleviate the odd languid heat that was flowing through her. Instead, she began to wonder if the hair on his chest was as red and silky as his beard. She shook her head to try to clear it. "I believe you," she said with a laugh that was a bit husky. "But hadn't we better keep going? I don't see how you're going to prevent my being hurt," she said, her eyes twinkling with mischief. "Not with your ass shot off."

He gave her a hug that was like being embraced by an affectionate grizzly bear. Lord, he was a big man.

"We'll make every effort to keep that from happening. I have a great fondness for that portion of my anatomy." Then he released her and started hustling her through the underbrush at a pace that gave neither of them breath for further conversation.

Zilah's lungs felt as if they were about to burst, and her jeans and shirt were as wet with perspiration as if she'd been dropped into a lake. Oh, dear, she wished she hadn't thought of that simile. Being immersed in a cool mountain lake was the stuff dreams were made of at this particular moment.

Daniel cast her a glance over his shoulder. His eyes narrowed to pierce the dusk that was falling around them. "All right?"

She nodded, saving her breath. She was going to need it. In the past few hours Daniel had set a grueling pace. She didn't know how many miles they had come, but if sheer exhaustion was any measure, it must have been a hundred. These hills had looked so cool and inviting when she'd first caught sight of them. That misty coolness had truly been the mirage she had thought it. Here in the shade of the trees it was only a few degrees cooler than the desert.

"I'll let you rest soon," Daniel said. "I want to make it down to the foothills before dark." He didn't wait for an answer but turned and set off again. His long, powerful legs traversed the downhill slope with a speed and surety that was amazing in a man so large. He moved very silently as well, she thought as she forced herself to try to match that torturous pace. Was his stealth responsible for his managing to plant all those charges around the plane without being detected? Must be, she decided. Now he had to be feeling the heat as she was. His khaki shirt was plastered to his back and arms, and that backpack and rifle he was carrying had to be suffocatingly hot as well as heavy. Yet he wasn't even breathing hard, darn it. She was ready to drop in her tracks and he looked like he was out for a leisurely stroll.

He stopped so short she almost ran into him. "Come on. I thought I remembered it being here." He took her arm and half pulled her up a sloping knoll that bordered the downhill path. "It's just around this little cliff."

"What is?"

"A small cave, and down the hill a little farther is a tiny stream. We can shelter there for the night."

"We're not going to go on?"

"Hassan and his boys may be combing the hills, and I don't want to blunder into them in the dark. Not with you along. We're close enough to the border that we can reach it in a few hours. We'll start out again before dawn." He pulled her up the last few yards. His arm encircled her waist as he half carried her over the overgrown path around the knoll.

"You don't have to stop on my account," she said, trying to catch her breath. "I'm fine."

He glanced down at her, and for an instant his hand on her waist tightened imperceptibly. "I can see that," he said gruffly. "You look as if you're ready to collapse at any moment, but you're just fine. You can handle it, right?"

She grinned. "Right." She felt a surge of warmth that was different from the hot tingling she had felt before. This was more comforting, as sweetly soothing as her mother's touch, even David's touch. How strange that this stranger could fill her with such a tempestuous mixture of emotions. "I can handle it."

"Well, you're not going to have to handle anything at the moment." They emerged from the shrubbery on the other side of the knoll, and he stopped in front of a small opening in the side of the hill that was no more than five feet in circumference.

"That's your cave?" She shook her head. "I think I prefer to stay out here for the night. I don't like confined places, and that looks awfully small."

"It goes back fifty yards or so. You'll be safe in there once I scrounge up some ground cover to hide the opening." He grimaced. "I don't like the idea any better than you do. I have a thing about closed-in places too."

"Then why not stay out here?"

"Because it's safer for you in the cave," he said curtly. "Stay here. I'm going to take a look inside. I don't like unpleasant surprises."

The mouth of the cave looked dark and menacing in the fast-falling twilight. "Are there any bears in Said Ababa?" she asked.

"Not that I know of." Daniel leaned his rifle against the wall of the cliff beside the cave opening, unstrapped his backpack, and dropped it to the ground. "I was thinking more on the line of bats and spiders."

"Bats!" She shivered. "I think I'd rather face a bear."

"Well, with any luck you won't have to face either one." He had drawn a small penlight from his backpack and was on his knees, starting to crawl through the low opening. "Though I do think it would be a good idea to examine your priorities in that area."

He seemed to be gone a terribly long time. Dear heaven, she hated just standing there waiting helplessly while Daniel took the initiative. Why hadn't she insisted on going with him? He had been risking his life for her from the moment he had walked into the cabin of the plane she'd been held hostage on, and she was still letting him run risks. That hole looked so dark and creepy.

Snakes! What if there were snakes in there?

She wasn't even aware that she had dropped to her knees until she had crawled halfway through the opening. Oh, dear heaven, it was dark in here. And she could hear no sound in the darkness ahead.

"Daniel?" It came out as a whispering quaver, she noticed in disgust. What a miserable coward she was being. She lowered her head, took a deep breath, and began to crawl forward as fast as she could.

Suddenly her head ran into something

solid with a force that made her see stars. She lifted her head swiftly in alarm and she rammed into something equally hard. A chin?

"Ouch!" It was a pained grunt from the bulk in front of her, followed by a shockingly explicit curse.

"Daniel?"

"Who else would it be, for heaven's sake? What the devil are you doing in here? Besides trying to knock me unconscious, that is."

"I was worried about you." She found her arms clutching at him desperately. "Snakes."

"What?"

"There might be snakes in here." He was so big and warm and safe. She had slithered forward and now his arms were holding her. She could hear his heart beating beneath her ear, filling the darkness with its vitality. "Why isn't your flashlight on?"

"I was saving the batteries. I don't have extra batteries for this one and we may need it later. I used it to check out all the nooks and crannies and then turned it off for the crawl back to the opening." His hands were moving over her shoulders and back in a caress that was sexless, she could tell. Yet his touch was causing hot vibrations to spread to her every nerve ending. "Didn't it

54

occur to you that if you were afraid, it would be smarter not to come crawling to my rescue?"

She shook her head. "If you're afraid of something, you have to confront it. I found that out a long time ago. If you hide your head, it festers inside of you until it poisons you. I had to come."

His hands stopped their soothing caress for an instant. "Yes, I think you did." His lips brushed the top of her head with a feather-light kiss. "You'll be glad to know that your attempt to rescue me wasn't necessary. No snakes. No bats. No bears." He pushed her gently away. "Now, suppose you turn around and crawl out of here? I have a craving for fresh air. This place is smaller than I remembered." He turned her around and gave her derriere an encouraging pat. "Move."

The air smelled clean and sweet despite its heavy heat when she crawled out of the cave. She shifted away from the opening and settled herself with a sigh of relief against the hard stone of the cliff wall. Daniel was close behind and rested beside her. He pulled a pack of cigarettes from his shirt pocket and lit one before leaning back against the cliff and inhaling deeply. "Oh, sorry." He fumbled for the crumpled pack he had jammed back into his shirt pocket. "Would you like one?"

She shook her head. "I don't smoke."

"Would you rather I didn't?"

"No, I don't mind people around me smoking. I just can't stand the thought of it myself." She closed her eyes and arched her throat to let the fresh breeze touch her with its sweet freedom.

"Disease?"

She shook her head. "No, it's the dependency. I can't bear the idea of becoming addicted to them. It frightens me."

"Frightens you?" Daniel's brow arched quizzically. "That's rather strange in a girl who isn't afraid of bears, terrorists, or snakes."

She opened her eyes. "Is it?" She was suddenly rising to her feet. "Did you say there was a creek nearby?"

"At the bottom of the hill in that little cluster of tamarisk trees." He could scarcely see her face in the dimness of the dusk, but her shoulders were oddly rigid and tense. He slowly crushed out his cigarette on the ground. "Wait a minute and I'll show you."

"No, that's all right. I'll find it." She was already hurrying, almost running down the hill.

Daniel muttered a low exclamation as he

got to his feet and followed more slowly. The woman changed moods from moment to moment. One second she was a frightened little girl, clinging to him in the darkness, the next she was coolly strong and mature. And now she was acting as nervous as that high-strung palomino she had been riding in the photograph. If he had to form an instant obsession with any woman, why couldn't it be with one who wasn't as complicated as that Mah-Jongg game Philip was so fanatic about? He had only known the woman one afternoon and she had already aroused in him an entire gamut of emotions. Desire, tenderness, protectiveness, jealousy. If he hadn't been so jealous of her precious David, he'd have been a hell of a lot more diplomatic about staking his claim. He could tell he had almost scared her to death. Not that he wouldn't have established his possession before he turned her over to Clancy anyway. From the minute he had sat down across from her on the plane he had known. It was like the pieces of a puzzle at last slipping into place. God, it had felt weird.

He frowned as he crossed the last few yards to the tamarisk grove. Zilah must think *he* was the weird one: An ex-mercenary with the edges still rough and unpolished, barging into her life, throwing bombs around and telling her that she was going to belong to him whether she liked it or not. It was no wonder she was acting so skittish.

He would have to curb his impatience and be gentle and civilized. Hell, she was only twenty-one. A college kid who had probably been sheltered from rough bastards like him. What had he been doing when he was twenty-one? Nam and then central Africa and then . . . He couldn't even remember all the countries, all the wars, all the women he had gone through in all those years that separated them. He'd have to be very careful to keep those years and experiences from intruding between them. Yes, he'd be very discreet and cool from now on and maybe . . .

All thoughts of coolness and discretion fled as he caught sight of her kneeling on the stones that banked the rushing creek. She had taken off her cotton shirt and the straps of her lacy bra were pushed down on her arms as she bathed her face and shoulders with a white handkerchief. It was the same handkerchief he had given her on the plane, he realized. Her sunstreaked hair was falling in a straight silky cloak around her. One hand reached up to push the shimmering mass over her shoulder and it rippled down her back. She dipped the handkerchief in the water again and wrung out the bit of cotton before running it in slow enjoyment down her arm from shoulder to wrist.

Daniel inhaled sharply. He felt as if that leisurely hand was stroking *his* body, not her own. His loins ached. He could imagine her hand moving so caressingly over him. A pulse hammered in his temple and a heavy heat spread over him in waves of sheer lust.

He hadn't made a sound, but she must have felt his presence, for her head turned toward him like that of a startled deer. She went still. Then, when she recognized him in the shadows, she laughed shakily. "I must be more nervous than I thought. You frightened me." The tenseness flowed out of her. She bent over the stream to dip her improvised washcloth once more into the water. "This feels wonderful. I'll let you have your handkerchief back in a moment, but if I don't get some of this sand and sweat off me, I'm going to perish."

"Take your time." His voice was hoarse, almost guttural, and there was tension about his massive shadow that generated a matching nervousness within her. She couldn't decipher his expression in the dusk, but she could feel his gaze on her. She was suddenly conscious of her partial nudity and had the impulse to scramble hurriedly back into her shirt. How very stupid! She was wearing more than she customarily did on the beach and they were in a situation where practicality, not modesty should prevail. "I wish I had something else to wear," she said with forced cheerfulness.

"I have another shirt in my backpack that you can have." He was moving slowly toward her. "It will probably come down to your knees but at least it's clean." He paused beside her, looming over her like a solid wall. "I'll go and get it."

She shook her head. "Then *you* won't have anything to wear. I've taken too much from you already." She tilted her head to gaze up at him. "I'm very grateful, you know. I don't think I told you that."

"I don't want your gratitude." He dropped to his knees beside her. "I'm going to want a hell of a lot of things from you, but gratitude isn't one of them." He laid his rifle on the ground beside him. His fingers were rapidly unbuttoning his shirt and stripping it off. Then he was bending over the creek, delving into the water and scrubbing his face and throat with the energy that characterized his every movement. The bronzed muscles of his shoulders and back were rippling and sliding as he moved, and her gaze clung to him compulsively. He wasn't really handsome by any conventional standard. There was no reason for her to get this breathless and to be unable to look away from him. Virile magnetism and the muscular grace of a Roman gladiator were all he possessed. All? It was more than enough to make her knees go weak and cause her hands to shake so badly that she could hardly hold on to the handkerchief.

He was splashing the cool water on the cloud of fiery hair on his chest now, and she could see the water beading on his flesh. She had a sudden impulse to lean forward and lick the drops away. The thought sent a thrill of pure shock through her. Desire. Despite the assurance of the psychiatrist she'd been seeing every week for the past six years, she had never believed she would experience that particular emotion. Yet how could this primitive yearning be anything else?

She could feel her breasts swell, their peaks hardening in an incredible response. She wanted to cover that response with her hands, but that would have been too revealing an action. She snatched up her shirt instead.

"No!"

Her eyes widened and flew swiftly to his face.

His gaze was on her full breasts veiled only by the sheer lace of the bra she wore. His face was heavy with a sensuality that made her catch her breath. "Not yet," he said huskily. "Come here."

Her tongue moistened her lips. "I don't think that would be a good idea. This situation is so . . . extraordinary that our reactions are a little out of kilter."

"Yours may only be out of kilter, but mine are going crazy." His finger reached out to touch the betraying prominence of one nipple through the lace of her bra. "And I think you're progressing nicely in the same direction."

She flinched back. It was as if she were being stroked with electricity when he touched her so lightly.

He smiled crookedly. "See?" His hands cupped her shoulders gently. "Pretty explosive, isn't it?"

"All the more reason . . ." He was pulling her into his embrace and she was yielding like a bit of metal to a magnet. Why wasn't she struggling? Then she was pressed against the warm hardness of his chest and she forgot about questions. His fiery mat of hair was stroking her woman's softness with flames of sensation. Her head was swimming and she couldn't seem to get her breath. She trustingly rested her cheek against him with a little sigh. "This is a mistake, Daniel. It's too soon. We don't know anything about each other."

"We'll find out everything we need to know." His fingers were tangled in her hair as he pulled her head back to look into her eyes. The expression emanating from his own eyes was grave. "Just a little now. I won't ask more than you want to give." He shook his head ruefully. "Five minutes ago I was promising myself I'd be very cool and patient. Now all I can do is promise I won't throw you down and rape you." He lowered his head slowly. "I want to be so gentle with you, Zilah. I've never felt this way before. I usually like it hard and fast, but not with you." His warm breath was feathering her lips. "I want to savor every touch." The first brush of his lips was so light she scarcely felt it. Then he captured, held, and cherished her. His lips moved, brushed, angled as one caress became a hundred. Taking breath and warmth and yet giving more back than he took.

How lovely, Zilah thought dreamily as her hands moved to caress his shoulders. He was so smooth and warm. So strong to be so gentle. It was all so new. As if each kiss, each touch were being created at this magic moment. How did he manage to create sorcery like that?

"Zilah."

"Hmmm."

"Open your lips, love. I want to taste you." His fingers were combing through her hair with tactile sensuality while he coaxed her lips apart. "Don't you want to taste me too?"

"Yes." She wanted to taste everything about him, touch every part of him, with a hunger that amazed her. Then his tongue was warm on her lips, lazily brushing, before he plunged inside, exploring her teeth, toying playfully with her tongue. It was an intimacy performed so lovingly that it became surprisingly natural, even comfortable. She almost laughed aloud when that thought filtered through the sensual haze Daniel was weaving about her. How could she be so aware in every throbbing pore and still think it comfortable, for heaven's sake?

Daniel's hands were fumbling beneath her hair and she felt a sudden loosening. Then he was slipping the straps of her bra off her arms while his lips covered hers. Flesh to flesh, warmth to warmth, hard muscle against the soft cushion of her breasts. A wrenching ache began throbbing between her thighs. "Oh, Zilah, isn't this great, love?" He pushed her away to look down at her. "It's getting too dark to see you, dammit." He gave her a swift, hard kiss. "Come on." He was on his feet, his hand grasping hers and pulling her to her feet.

"Where are we going?" she asked, startled.

He draped his discarded shirt around her carefully before picking up his rifle and her bra and blouse. "Back to the cave," he said. "I can't see you in the dark and I won't risk your neck and mine making love to you out here in the open."

"Is that what you were doing?" she asked quietly.

"Making love?" He shot her a glance. "You're damn right I was making love to you. If I was just using you sexually you'd know it, Zilah. I'm not very subtle."

She suddenly giggled, feeling ridiculously light-headed. "Hard and fast?"

"Right." His hand was at her waist, propelling her up the hill. "With lots of fireworks. You'll like it like that, too, I hope, but we'll start out slow and easy."

She stiffened and was silent for a long moment. "I don't think I'm ready for . . . fireworks," she said hesitantly. "This has come as something of a surprise to me."

65

He didn't answer until they had reached the mouth of the cave. "Like I said, we'll keep it slow and easy. Right now I kind of like the idea of courting you." His grasp tightened on her waist. "Just don't try to shut me out entirely. I couldn't stand it after touching you. I'll do without the Roman candles, but a few firecrackers are required."

She had an idea she would have a difficult time resisting the temptation to touch Daniel as well in the future. "Whatever you say," she said meekly.

He snorted inelegantly. "As long as it's what you want too." His voice became unexpectedly grim. "Honesty, Zilah. There has to be absolute honesty between us. Tell me it's what you want too."

"It's what I want too, Daniel," she said quietly. And it was, she realized with amazement. He had only to touch her and she wanted him so much that it shook her to her foundations. "It's exactly what I want."

His arm tightened in a quick hug. "That's my girl." He released her and turned away. "Now, why don't you rummage in my backpack to find that clean shirt. I'll go and see what I can do about rustling up some shrubbery to cover the cave opening."

Zilah watched him stride away in a state bordering on bemusement. He had stirred so many responses in her with his vibrant presence that now she felt suddenly cold and a little lost. She gave herself a shake and deliberately turned her eyes away from Daniel's lithe retreating back.

He was a stranger, blast it. She couldn't possibly be so emotionally involved with a stranger. His dynamic vitality and bold, rakish charm had merely captured her imagination. His sexual attraction for her had caught her off guard and she mustn't mistake chemistry for something deeper. A man like Daniel must have eager women standing in line to crawl into his bed. How could she compete with them when she didn't even know if she could respond sexually to any man? Yet Daniel wasn't just any man. She had melted like a snowball tossed into a bonfire when he had touched her — that was the final healing, according to Dr. Melrose. He had been so coolly clinical when he had made his recommendation to respond freely if she ever did feel that flare of sexual attraction. The possibility had seemed so remote that she had listened indifferently at the time, but now . . . What if Daniel were offering her nothing but a physical rapport that might last only a few weeks? If he took from her, he might also be giving more than he could ever imagine. The final healing that would make her a whole woman at last.

She dropped to her knees on the ground beside the backpack, her fingers fumbling at the straps. She instinctively shied away from the realization of what that healing would bring. She wouldn't think, she would only feel while she was with Daniel. She would flow with the tide. She could rely on him to see that she wouldn't drown in that sea of emotion. There was a warm sensitivity beneath his surface hardness that she intuitively trusted.

She swiftly shed the shirt Daniel had draped around her shoulders and slipped on the blue cotton workshirt from the backpack. It felt crisp and clean against her skin and smelled faintly of lime and tobacco. She rummaged through the backpack. There was bread and cheese wrapped in a cloth, a large battery-operated lantern together with a packet of extra batteries, a white undershirt, a box of ammunition for the rifle, a folded silver-coated sheet, a wicked-looking machete. In all, a very workmanlike, efficient emergency backpack. Like Daniel himself: Practical, lethal, and efficient.

"Pass me that machete, will you?" Daniel asked from behind her. He unslung his rifle and handed it to her in exchange for the machete. "I've found a dead tree we can use. It will take only fifteen or twenty minutes to drag up enough branches to cover the opening."

"May I help?"

"No, you stay here." He turned back as a thought struck him. "Do you know how to use this rifle?"

"I'm pretty good with a Browning automatic. David's father taught me how to shoot at the ranch. I don't know how I'd get along with this one." She made a face. "This is one of those rifles that doubles as a machine-gun, isn't it?"

He nodded. "An M-1. You just adjust the cartridge lever and pull the trigger back." He turned away again. "Keep a sharp eye, Annie Oakley. I'll be back soon."

3

There was no way the interior of the cave could be made to appear inviting. But with the silvery camping sheet covering the rocky floor and the large utility lantern lit, it wasn't quite as frightening as before. However, nothing could take away the air of claustophrobic closeness of the small area.

"Zilah, dammit, where are you?" Daniel's voice outside the cave held both exasperation and a trace of panic.

"In here," she called as she laid out the bread and cheese on the silver sheet. "Dinner is served. Though I'd definitely prefer it al fresco. Are you sure we can't forget about this darn cave and sleep outside? I don't like it."

"I'm sure," he said curtly. He was crawling through the opening and suddenly the cave seemed even smaller. "I've camouflaged the entrance pretty thoroughly. It should be hidden from view unless someone is right on top of it." He had reached the sheet now and sat down tailor-fashion opposite her.

"Can we keep the lantern on? It makes it a little more cheerful."

"For a little while. I brought some spare batteries for it."

"I noticed." She picked up a flat piece of bread and took a bite. It was a little dry but the texture was satisfying. "Are you always so well equipped when you go on one of these assignments?"

"Always. I learned a long time ago you have to be prepared for the unexpected to happen. It usually does." He moved his shoulders as if to shrug off a weight. "God, it's close in here."

"That's what I said, if you'll recall." She took another bite of bread. "I'd be much happier outside."

"But not safer. You're better off here." He picked up a slice of the goat cheese. "We'll just have to forget about it. Talk to me. Did you like living on that ranch in Texas?"

"Oh, yes, it was wonderful," she said softly. "I'd never been to the country before David sent me there. I'd spent my entire childhood with my grandmother in Marasef and knew nothing but city life. I loved the space and the freedom. I could breathe

71

there." Her expression was suddenly alive with eagerness. "And the horses. I loved the horses. Jess gave me the loveliest palomino for my eighteenth birthday."

"Jess?"

"David's father. He taught me to ride and to rope and . . ."

"Where was your David during all this activity?"

"In Sedikhan. He and Billie have visited with us a few times since I left Zalandan, but their home is here." The eagerness in her face suddenly faded. "I was telling you the truth, you know. David is my friend, not my lover. Do you believe me?"

"I believe you." His lips twisted. "Maybe because I want to so damn much. You have to admit it's an odd set-up though. How many men would acquire a fourteen-year-old 'protégée' without ulterior motives? Particularly one who looks like you. What did your mother say about his whisking you out of the country?"

"She wasn't happy, but she realized it was for the best." Her eyes dropped to the silver sheet and her words came haltingly. "I was very ill at the time. They thought I'd do better in Texas."

"Ill?"

She nodded. "But I'm well now." She

glanced quickly at the uneaten slice of cheese in his hand. "You're not eating. Aren't you hungry?"

"Not very." He picked up the canteen and took a swallow of water. "Being surrounded by walls makes me edgy. It's a little quirk of mine." He offered the canteen to her, and when she shook her head, he recapped it and set it down. "Are you finished?"

"Yes." She was carefully rewrapping the bread and cheese. "I've had enough. Hassan gave me some fruit this morning for breakfast." She frowned worriedly. "You think they're out there searching for us?"

"Definitely."

She made a face. "Honesty is all very well, but I could have used a little comforting prevarication at the moment."

"Prevarication, no, comfort, yes." He rose to his knees and pulled her swiftly into his arms. "I could use a little comfort myself." His lips were nuzzling at her throat. "You feel like velvet and you taste . . ." His tongue licked delicately at the pulse in her throat. "Delicious."

She chuckled. "Is this what you categorize as comfort?" He nipped gently at the soft flesh beneath her chin and she felt an odd throbbing start in the tips of her breasts as if he'd pulled a secret erotic wire. "It doesn't feel very comfortable to me."

"Then you'll have to settle for pleasant." There was a flicker of mischief in the glance he gave her. "You have to admit that this is quite pleasant." His big hands were suddenly cupping her breasts, weighing and toying with them through the cotton of the shirt. She gasped and she could hear him give a low laugh. "Pleasant?"

"Remind me to buy you a dictionary," she whispered. "That's not the right word either."

His index finger was tracing the whorl of her nipple through the shirt, and she could feel herself hardening and peaking more with each circle of that teasing fingertip.

"It's only a question of comparison. What I'm doing to you now is only pleasant" — his finger inserted itself between the buttons of her shirt with shocking suddenness — "when you compare it to this."

The touch of his skin against her nipple sent heat rocketing through her. His finger was rubbing back and forth against the naked peak, then began flicking it with a fingernail with every pass. "What word would your dictionary use to describe this, Zilah?"

There weren't any words. She was being jolted by tremors with each tantalizing touch. "Daniel . . ."

His navy blue eyes were narrowed with satisfaction on her face. "You like that, don't you? I love that expression on your face; I love to know that what I'm doing is causing it."

Then his hands were rapidly unbuttoning her shirt and pushing it down her arms until it fell to the silver mat. "Ah, that's what I wanted." His eyes were caressing her with the same magic as his hands. "Lovely. All gold and pink and touched with warmth." He brought her close, rubbing her naked breasts sensually against the cloud of auburn hair on his chest. "My lovely summer girl."

"What?" she asked dazedly.

"Never mind," he muttered. His head was bent, his tongue gently stroking her nipple. She felt a white-hot shiver run through her. His lips closed on her with a strong suction that caused her back to arch and a low cry to break from her throat.

He lifted his head and drew a long, shaky breath. "Dear heaven, I want to be inside you. I want to hear you cry out like that when I come into you and fill you. I want to move and twist until every part of you belongs to me. To feel you tighten and pull at me."

"Daniel!"

He shook his head as if to clear it. "I think we were pretty close to sending up a few Roman candles." He grinned. "I never did like fooling around with the little stuff."

"I gathered that" — her heart was pounding so hard she could scarcely speak — "from your conversation."

"I told you I wasn't subtle." He suddenly frowned in concern. "I tend to get a bit graphic on occasion. Did I offend you?"

"No." He had excited her. She drew a shaky breath. "You didn't offend me."

His eyes were narrowed shrewdly on her face. "You liked it." He smiled. "And you like me. We fit, don't we, love?"

"Yes, I think perhaps we do." She returned his smile and then her breath abruptly caught in her throat as she met his eyes. The world narrowed down to just the two of them in a dark intimacy that glowed with all manner of starlike things. She pulled her gaze away with an effort. "I guess I'm not much on subtlety either."

"Lie down."

Her eyes flew to his in surprise.

He smiled slightly and shook his head. "No Roman candles, not even any firecrackers. Just you sleeping in my arms. I think we'd both like that. Okay?"

She nodded, her throat tight. "Okay." His

chest was warm and solid and the soft mat cushioned her naked back as he turned her spoon fashion, his palms lovingly cupping her breasts. Her hair splayed in a silken mass over his upper arm.

Treasured. The word came to her even as weariness flowed over her in an irresistible tide. Desire was still there, smoldering low, but it was that blessed feeling of being treasured that she was most conscious of now. Considering that he was a dangerous man who had exploded into her life with shocking violence, she was astounded that she should feel this way in his arms. Treasured and protected and . . .

She awoke to darkness and the uneasy feeling that something was wrong. Yet what could be wrong? she wondered drowsily. Daniel's arms were still around her, holding her securely, his warm breath feathering her ear. Her forehead knitted in a frown as she realized what was wrong. Daniel's breathing was jerky and labored and his arms around her were shaking. He was trembling as if he were a malaria victim! The panic that thought engendered jolted her wide awake.

"Daniel?" She tried to sit up but his arms were suddenly rigid manacles around her. "What's wrong?"

"Nothing's wrong." The words were jerky, as if they were spoken between clenched teeth. "Go back to sleep."

"There *is* something wrong," she insisted. "Are you ill?"

He laughed shortly. "If you can call being gutless ill, then I guess I am."

"Gutless? I don't know what you're talking about." Her concern was growing by the second. "Daniel, what's wrong? Dammit, you're scaring me."

He drew a deep breath. "God knows I didn't want to do that. Look, there's nothing to be afraid about. It's just my damn nerves. I told you I didn't like walls around me. I thought I had it under control, but I woke up and there it was gibbering at me in the darkness. Sometimes it happens like that. I'll be all right in a few minutes. Go back to sleep."

"Let me go, Daniel. I'm not going to go meekly back to sleep and leave you like this. I couldn't do that." She felt a slight loosening of his arms and she turned over to face him. Her arms slipped about his waist with an instinctive maternal protectiveness as old as time. "Now, what's wrong? Tell me."

The darkness was complete. It both isolated and bound them together with an unbelievable intimacy. It must be like this

78

floating in space, she thought vaguely as her hands began to soothingly stroke the tense slide of muscles that corded Daniel's back and shoulders.

"Why?" she asked softly. "If you suffer this badly from claustrophobia, why the devil are we here in this cave?"

"I told you why." His lips were buried in her hair, and the words were scarcely audible. He was obviously trying to stifle the trembling that was wracking his body, but an occasional shiver still shook him. "There's no way I'm going to make a bad situation riskier because of this damn weakness." He was speaking through set teeth. "It's been years since it happened. I thought I could control it."

"Since what happened?"

"A number of years ago I found myself thrown by a revolutionary group into a sod hut about the size of a postage stamp in the middle of the desert. It was six months before Clancy blew the group and got me out. My nerves were in pretty bad shape, so I left Sedikhan for a few years. I batted around the world for a while as captain of a schooner and then came back to work for Clancy."

"You were a sea captain?" Zilah's eyes were wide with curiosity.

"There weren't any walls," he said simply. "I needed that."

She felt a rush of sympathy so strong that she couldn't prevent helpless tears from forming in her eyes, and she couldn't speak for a moment without revealing the pity she felt. She hated pity herself and she could see that he detested revealing his weakness. Despite his offhand explanation, those few words had drawn a graphic picture that made her shudder. How terrible it must have been for a man of Daniel's temperament to be caged for that length of time. It was clear he was still feeling the effects even after all these years. Yet he hadn't hesitated to undergo an experience that he knew would be excruciatingly painful just to make life safer for her. "I can see how you would," she said huskily. "But what an idiotic man you are, Daniel Seifert." Her arms tightened instinctively around him. He had stopped shaking, but the muscles of his back and shoulders were rock-hard with tension. Her hands moved over them, trying to massage and release the tautness. "It's all right now. Go to sleep. I won't let you go. I'll hold you until morning."

"Will you?" His laugh held a touch of desperation. "I don't think that would be a very good idea. Not now." She could hear the leaping cadence of his heart beneath her ear, and the hard flesh of his chest was burning her cheek. "I'm not in control at the moment."

"None of us is in control all of the time. It's nothing to be ashamed of. Let me help you," she said softly. "You've done so much for me. I need to give to you too. Let me comfort you, Daniel."

"The kind of comfort I need now isn't the kind you have in mind." His words were muffled in her hair. She could feel his warm breath feathering her ear. "And you don't owe me anything, dammit. How many times do I have to tell you?" His chest was moving unevenly with the heaviness of his breathing. "Let me go, Zilah."

"No, I want to help you," she said calmly. "Tell me how I can best do that."

"Zilah, for God's sake, shut up," he gritted out through his teeth. "Do I have to spell it out for you? If you don't get away from me in about two minutes I'm going to have your clothes off and be inside you." His hands suddenly cupped her buttocks and brought her forcefully against his hard arousal. "I went to sleep wanting you and woke up with all the barriers down." His words were coming in little gasps as he rubbed her against him with a slow, sensual tempo that caused a hot flowering deep within her. "All I can think of is how you'd feel around me, the way your nipples hardened when my tongue touched them." His hands were clenching and releasing her buttocks as he spoke. She could feel her naked breasts swelling and firming against the hard wall of his chest as if on command. It was a command, she realized hazily, the most basic known to male and female. The soft pelt of hair on his chest was moving against her bare skin with the ragged tempo of his breathing, teasing, inciting, readying her for the next intimacy. "I want to feel you naked against me, to open your thighs and touch you. I want to make you melt and flow." His teeth suddenly clamped down on the lobe of her ear with a force that was almost painful. "Stop me, dammit," he growled desperately. "Because, God knows, I can't stop myself."

The darkness was swimming around her like ebony waters of forgetfulness where nothing existed but touch and sensation and Daniel's need crying out to her. And not only Daniel's need, she realized with a little shock. She needed him with a fierceness that was as primitive as that first instinctive maternal craving to give comfort. How could that be when . . . The doubts and questions flowed away into the darkness as she felt Daniel tremble against her. Not with fear but with desire. It was like being caught in the funnel of a tornado and being swept away from everything she had ever known. The only things that were real were the sensations Daniel was provoking with every word, every touch.

"I don't think I can stop you either," she said faintly. "I don't think I even want to."

He went still. "Oh, Lord, I wish you hadn't said that."

She hadn't thought the muscles beneath her hands could become harder, but they did. His entire body was gathering charges of tension like lightning about to strike. "I didn't want it to be like this. I wanted to show you that I could be something besides a roughneck who knows only how to take." His hands were suddenly working swiftly, feverishly, at the zipper of her jeans. "I don't even know if I can be gentle with you."

"You don't have to be gentle." It wouldn't matter. Not with Daniel. She wanted to give him whatever he wanted. Fill every need before he asked. He was stripping away her jeans and the panties beneath them with frantic urgency, and then she was naked in the darkness. His hands were running over her body as if he couldn't get enough of the textures of her. He squeezed the softness of her breasts in his two big hands, then moved down her rib cage in a long, lingering caress. His fingers were hard and callused as they brushed against her softness. Sandpaper and silk. She felt every nerve and pore come alive in a tingling rush as he touched her and then moved on, lingering on her navel to playfully insert a finger while he patted her stomach with the other hand. Then his hand was tangling in the curls that guarded her womanhood, tugging gently. "Open for me," he said thickly. "Please, Zilah. I can't wait anymore. Let me come in."

She didn't think she could wait either. How could darkness so intense hold fingers of flames and curling blossoms of fire that took her breath and made her mindless with pleasure? Her thighs opened with languid invitation that was purely instinctive. Command, response, reward.

Reward. She inhaled sharply as she received a blindingly sensual reward for obedience when his hands touched her with a probing intimacy that sent a shock of desire twisting through her.

"You're so warm and sweet down here," Daniel muttered. "I wish I could see you. I'd light the lantern but I don't think I can wait a minute longer." His finger suddenly found the soft sensual trigger he'd been seeking, and he began a rotating massage that brought a soft cry from her.

Her hips lifted in an offering that was as old as time. His husky laugh held an element of satisfaction. "You want me? Now, Zilah?"

"Now." She could barely get the word past the tightness in her throat. She was on fire. Every breath was difficult to the point of pain. Her head was thrashing back and forth on the slickness of the silver sheet in mindless aching need. Darkness, touch, flame.

"Good." The word held a guttural urgency that was totally male. She was vaguely aware that the touch was gone. Only the darkness, and the throbbing, flaming need remained as Daniel moved with frantic swiftness to strip off the remainder of his clothes.

She was shivering with hunger. Aching with emptiness. She could feel the muscles of her stomach clench and knot, pleading for the touch she had known so briefly.

Then the touch was back, parting her thighs, stroking her gently, opening her with an eagerness that held a hint of restrained savagery. He was between her thighs. The powerful muscles that corded his own thighs were taut against her softness. She couldn't see his bulk looming above her and somehow that only added to the erotic excitement. She could see only in her mind's eye the pelt of auburn hair that covered his chest, the sensual heaviness of his face, the sheer massive size of him that made her feel small and helpless in comparison. She couldn't see him but she could feel him nudging against the heart of her. For an instant there was a flicker of memory that caused her to tense. Then it was gone. Because there wasn't anything in the past that bore the slightest resemblance to what she was experiencing now. New. Everything was new and clean and as basic as if it were happening at the dawn of time. Daniel's magic again.

He was entering her carefully, trying not to hurt her with his sheer size. She could sense the care, the agonizing tension in him. His breath was coming in little rasps. He was trying to give her the gentleness he thought she wanted, she realized with a rush of tenderness. Even though the restraint was hurting him, he was trying to give to her. Well, she wanted to give to him also. Give and give until there was nothing left to offer. Hard and fast. He had said he liked it hard and fast.

Her hands suddenly closed on his hips, her nails digging into the hard flesh. "Daniel." Her voice was a soft yearning murmur in the darkness. "Come." Her hips surged upward, taking him with a boldness that brought a low cry from his lips. She felt like uttering the same cry, but she was afraid he would mistake it for pain. So full. Stretched, complete and yet still throbbing with emptiness. "Come . . . to me." She could barely get the words out.

"Sweet heaven, Zilah." He shuddered. She could feel it within her, and it brought a quivering flutter to every nerve and limb. Together. How close they were. One flesh. "I'm going wild. I've never felt like this in my life. I'm afraid to let go. I'll hurt you, dammit."

"You won't hurt me." Her fingers tightened on his hips. "It's all right, Daniel."

"I hope so." She could feel the forces swirling about him in the darkness. Electricity gathering for the strike. "Because I can't stop myself now."

He plunged forward, wildness overcoming restraint as he took her with a force and beauty as hot and violent as the lightning to which she had mentally compared him. He was lifting her up to meet each strong thrust, grinding against her as if he wanted to reach beyond closeness to a unity that couldn't be broken as passion passed.

She was vaguely conscious that he was talking to her as he moved, telling her how sweet she was, how good she felt around him, of the other ways he was going to love her. His words were as hoarse and wild as the rhythm of his movements. Sometimes shockingly graphic, sometimes tender as a mother's kiss. She tried to help him, meet fire with fire, but once loosed, he overwhelmed her. It was like a tempest picking her up, tossing her from crest to crest, yet never letting her leave the center of power.

Lightning, power, strength that never conquered, beauty that never yielded. It couldn't go on. Yet it did. A moment. Forever. Darkness. Flame. Lightning again. A breathless shock that burned her to the core, then another, spreading, rippling in patterns of power. Daniel's power. So much power in one man, she thought feverishly. So much beauty and primitive need that — Then she could think no more as the lightning struck with a final blue-white force that absorbed the flame and the darkness and everything in the world except the man who wielded it.

She heard Daniel cry out and then felt the heavy weight of him upon her. His heart was beating so hard it appeared to be trying to burst from his chest. Or was that her own heartbeat? It was difficult to tell, so closely were they joined in body and spirit. He shifted off her and to the side, still holding her with possessive strength.

"Did I hurt you?" His question was gruff, but she could still detect the concern. "I didn't mean to be so rough. I think I went a little crazy."

Hurt? She didn't know if there'd been any pain or not. It had all been too world-shaking for her to separate the sensations she had been experiencing. She was conscious of a slight ache between her thighs now that Daniel had left her, but she wasn't certain whether it was soreness or an aching emptiness to be refilled. "You didn't hurt me."

"You're sure?" His palm reached between her thighs to rub her with loving gentleness. "You felt so good that I wanted to take every bit of you." His tone was rueful. "I think I tried to do just that. Next time I'll try to act more the gentleman. You can see I'm not used to the role."

"I didn't mind." The words were so inadequate. She felt tongue-tied, and the tears were stinging behind her closed lids. How could she tell him what a precious gift he had given her? The final healing. It had come so swiftly out of this darkness that had seemed suspended in time. Her own need to give comfort to Daniel had flowed effortlessly into the giving of her body as well. Giving. That was the key. It was being taken that was the horror. Giving was beautiful. Giving was love. Her lips curved in a smile of radiant tenderness invisible to him in the darkness. And Daniel had given her that beauty. He had been rough and passionate as a storm at sea yet he had still given as well as taken. Why was he worrying so about a roughness that she had instigated herself? "You were upset."

He stiffened. His hand ceased its intimate petting motion and dropped away from her. "And you felt sorry for me," he said with soft violence. "Dammit, you felt sorry for me!"

"No," she protested. "I mean, yes, I did feel sorry for you. I wanted to help you." He had rolled away from her, and she could hear him moving in the darkness, pulling on his clothes. "But that's not —"

"The hell it wasn't. You felt sorry for me." His voice was jerky. "My God, you even told me how grateful you were to me. So grateful you decided to give the guy a little tip for his trouble."

"A tip?" Zilah tried to smother the anger that flared at his choice of words. She sat up. "I don't give tips of that nature." Her voice was taut with pain. "Contrary to what you may think, I am not a whore."

"Oh, hell, I've done it again." The light of the lantern snapped on to reveal Daniel kneeling in front of her. He was dressed, with the exception of his shirt. His hair was a tousled mass of flame and his eyes were narrowed in concern on her face. "I've hurt your feelings, haven't I? I'm sorry. I guess my damn pride got in the way. I couldn't stand the thought of being a charity case. It brings back too many memories."

"Memories?"

The light of the lantern struck sleek shadows over his naked shoulders as he shrugged. "I was an orphan from the time I was six. I guarantee that it doesn't give you a liking for being on the receiving end." His gaze wandered down her body to rest with compulsive intensity on the soft velvet folds that his hand had so recently caressed. His tongue ran over his lips to moisten their sudden dryness. "On the other hand, there's a distinct possibility I could change my mind given the right set of circumstances. You're lovely, Zilah."

She felt a familiar tingling begin where his gaze was caressing her. "You're not very steadfast."

"Oh, but I am." His gaze flew back to her face, and he answered with surprising gravity. "I'm as steadfast as the North Star. Once my course is set, I don't change. Remember that."

She was caught up in those swirls of dark intimacy once again and for a moment she couldn't break free. She pulled her eyes away from his with an effort and lowered them to the glittering silver sheet on which they were sitting. "I'll remember." She felt suddenly shy. Strange after all they'd experienced together to feel this sudden rush of shyness. She reached for the blue shirt Daniel had taken off her earlier and slipped it on hurriedly. "I wasn't treating you like a charity case, you know. I just wanted to help." She lifted her eyes to meet his. "I still do." She drew a deep breath and turned away, snatching up her clothes and pulling them on quickly. "And I intend to do just that, whether you think it's charity or not. As I said before, you can be a very idiotic man, Daniel."

He frowned. "Idiotic? What the hell do you — What are you doing?"

She glanced up from where she was kneeling, stuffing items hastily in the backpack. "Packing up. We're getting out of here. Grab the sheet and the lantern, will you?" She was crawling toward the opening, dragging the backpack behind her.

"Zilah, dammit, come back here!"

"Not a chance," she said over her shoulder. "If you're so determined to keep me safe, you'll have to do it under an open sky." She heard him growl something under his breath but she ignored it serenely. By the time she had negotiated the barricade that Daniel had erected at the mouth of the cave he was right behind her. His expression was grim in the halo of light from the lantern. "This is crazy, Zilah. Get back into the cave."

"And lie awake worrying about you all night?" She shook her head. "You know that if I weren't along, you'd be taking your chances out here."

He went still. "Worrying about me?"

"Yes, worrying," she echoed softly. "I think I may be worrying quite a bit about you from now on, Daniel." She sat down and leaned her back against the stony wall of the cliff. "If you'll sit down and get settled, we'll be able to turn out the lantern. For someone who is so concerned about Hassan discovering us, you're being very reckless."

He dropped down beside her, still scowling. "Zilah, you're being —"

93

She swiftly put her fingers over his lips. "Shall I tell you something David Bradford once told me when I was going through a bad time? He said, 'I can't claim to understand your pain. We all experience sadness and pain in accordance with our own natures. But if you'll let me, I'll share it. Open to me, give to me, and we'll handle it together. That's how it should be between friends.' " Her eyes were glowing softly. "And we are friends, Daniel. Despite what happened in that cave tonight, I know I don't have any right to expect more from you. I don't want you to feel pressured or harried. I realize that I'm nothing special in your life, that you probably would have reacted to any woman in the same way. Sex hasn't as much emotional significance to a man as it does to a woman." She smiled a little shakily. "But we do have friendship. We couldn't have gone through what we did today without jumping a few hundred boundaries or so." She nestled her head on his shoulder with the endearing confidence of a small child. "So, like it or not, we're in this together, Daniel."

Daniel flipped off the lantern and was silent for a long moment. "I . . . do like it." His big hand gently began to stroke her hair. "Old friend."

"Good." She was vaguely conscious of his tucking the silver sheet over both of them. "Now, go to sleep and we'll worry about Hassan tomorrow."

"Yes, ma'am." There was a thread of amusement beneath the meekness in his voice.

It didn't disturb the contentment she was experiencing. How lovely to be needed, she thought drowsily. For the past few years she had been the one in constant need. Everyone around her had treated her as if she were a piece of fine china that had been shattered, and though repaired, must always be given special care. But with Daniel she could give as well as take. How wonderful to know that no matter how dominant and aggressive he appeared, there would be moments when Daniel needed her.

Zilah drifted off to sleep almost immediately but Daniel didn't even make the attempt. With the rifle within reach he felt fairly secure, but there was no way he would expose Zilah to additional risk. He would sit here until dawn and guard her while she slept. A slight smile touched his lips and he brushed a kiss on her temple. He would be careful to guard her very well.

Nothing special. Those were the words she had used to describe an experience that had rocked him to his foundations. She had tried so hard to be understanding and sophisticated: he had been torn between tenderness and indignation as she'd told him so gravely she knew that the sexual experience they'd shared meant little to him. Perhaps it hadn't been more than physical gratification in the past, but that was before Zilah. Before he had looked into clear, grave eyes that asked and answered at the same time. Before he had seen a summer smile that he knew would now hold all the seasons of loving for him.

Hell, he couldn't expect her to feel the same way. He had known that she was actually backing away from him when she'd been murmuring all that bull about how she didn't want him to feel harried. Who could blame her when he had just taken her with less ceremony and finesse than he usually spent on the most casual of bedmates? He had lost control and he'd been damned lucky she hadn't rejected him entirely. She needed breathing room, and if he wanted her to come to him willingly and joyfully, then he had to give it to her. Damn, it was going to be hard after having her tonight. He had been within a breath of making love to her again when she had bundled up their belongings and crawled out of the cave.

What a crazy thing to do. Crazy and sweet and caring.

He leaned his head back against the stone wall of the cliff and breathed in the sweet warm air that was scented pungently with wild grass and tamarisk. His arm tightened unconsciously about Zilah. He felt very lucky tonight. Luckier than ever before in his life. For the first time in years he was feeling an eager anticipation about what lay ahead, especially that moment when his friend was ready to acknowledge that he was also her lover.

4

It was still dark when Zilah opened her eyes. Daniel's arms were no longer around her, and she saw the dark blur of his large bulk looming over her.

"Is it time to get up?" she asked, yawning. "It's still pitch dark."

"Not for long. By the time we pack up and wash the sleep away it will be light enough to travel." Daniel was swiftly pulling on his sleeveless undershirt. "It will take over two hours to reach Sheikh El Kabbar's compound and I want to get there before the sun is high. Once we leave the hills we'll be in desert country again." He tossed the penlight onto her lap. "Why don't you go down to the creek while I repack the backpack?"

She stretched lazily. "I'll do that." She got to her feet, flinching as she felt the stiffness of her cramped muscles. "It may take a while to get my legs working. I'd better start right away." She turned on the flashlight, catching Daniel in its pool of light. As usual, his sheer size was a shock. His red hair was tousled and the low-necked sleeveless undershirt revealed a wisp of the auburn hair on his chest. Despite the explosive vitality that exuded from him, his face showed fatigue, especially in the deep lines at the corners of his eyes. "Didn't you sleep at all?"

He shook his head. "You're a very nice armful," he said lightly. "I decided I was enjoying myself too much to waste time sleeping." He inclined his head in a mocking bow. "I hope you'll forgive me for not obeying your orders, oh, *lallah.*"

"Much you care." She tried to smother a smile as she turned and started down the hill toward the tamarisk grove. She glanced back over her shoulder. "You're definitely not a team player, Daniel."

"Clancy would never have sent a team player on a mission like this," he drawled, his eyes twinkling. "And if he hadn't sent me, think of all we would have missed."

She chuckled. "Bombs exploding, being shot at, pursuit by terrorists. I have to admit it hasn't been dull. Life may seem a bit tame when this is over."

"Then I'll have to think of something to

liven things up a bit." He leered at her. "I have a few ideas in mind that might suffice. You forgot about the Roman candles."

She smiled softly. "No, I didn't. I have to admit your fireworks are pretty unforgettable, Daniel."

There was still a smile lingering on her lips when she reached the creek and knelt down on the flat rocks that bordered it. She seemed to have been smiling a great deal since Daniel had appeared in her life. How many years had it been since she'd known joie de vivre rising within her? She had thought that welling spring had been stilled forever by the experience that had changed everything for her. Contentment had seemed prize enough.

She used the handkerchief to wash her face and throat, thinking wistfully of thick terry-cloth towels and toothbrushes and hot showers. . . .

She screamed in agony.

The pain was so blinding, so overwhelming, that for an instant she didn't know where it was coming from. It was everywhere. It was wracking her entire body. She found herself sobbing helplessly.

"Zilah, for God's sake, what's happened?" Daniel was kneeling beside her. He grabbed the lantern and swung it in a wide arc around the grove, the M-1 ready in his other hand.

"I don't know." The tears were running down her face. "Pain!"

"Where?"

She tried to pierce the haze that was enveloping her and identify its source. "My ankle, the right one, I think." She clutched at his shoulders, her nails biting into his flesh. "Oh, I don't know! It *hurts,* Daniel."

"I know. I know. Shhh. I know." He was shifting the lantern, playing the light down her leg to her feet.

"Oh, God!"

"What is it?" His voice was so shocked that she fought the dizziness to look over his shoulder. Ugliness. She had never seen anything so ugly as the creature crawling up her jean-clad calf.

Then Daniel was using the barrel of the M-1 to brush the creature away. He ground it into the stones with the butt of the gun. He stood up, slung the rifle on his shoulder, and picked her up. He climbed swiftly up the hill toward the cave.

"It was a scorpion, wasn't it?" she whispered, closing her eyes. "He stung me."

"It was a scorpion," he conceded grimly. "They don't usually like to be so close to water. It must have crawled out from under one of those rocks."

"They're very poisonous, aren't they?" she asked, moistening her lips. "Am I going to die, Daniel?"

"No! God, no, sweetheart. Nothing's going to happen to you."

"Don't look now, but I think it's already happened." She felt light-headed, floating on waves of pain. "He was ugly."

"What?"

"The scorpion. He was so ugly."

"Shut up, Zilah," he said huskily. "You're going to be fine. Don't think about it." He set her down with her back to the wall of the cliff and knelt beside her. He rolled up the cuff of the jeans on her right leg and inhaled sharply. Her ankle was already swollen to almost twice its normal size. He quickly pulled off her tennis shoe and stripped off her white sock.

"Where is that handkerchief?" He didn't wait for an answer as he spied it still clenched in her hand and took it from her. "I'm going to have to make a tourniquet to keep the poison from spreading. Not very tight, just enough to slow the circulation a little. We'll keep a close watch on it and loosen it every so often." He was wrapping and tying the handkerchief directly above her ankle as he spoke. "The important thing is to keep the venom from spreading before we can get you to a doctor. The initial pain will ebb soon, but sometimes a fever follows. Don't be frightened if it does."

"You seem to know quite a bit about scorpion stings," Zilah said faintly. "Is that required instruction for Clancy's agents?"

"I learned this particular knowledge on my own," Daniel said as he rolled down the cuff of her jeans. "One of the favorite amusements of those bastards who held me in that shack was to throw a scorpion or snake into the room with me and watch me scramble to cope with it. After I got out I made it my business to know everything there was to know about poisonous vermin of all types. I never wanted to be that helpless again."

Poor Daniel. How horrible that experience must have been for him. And how many other experiences had he gone through that were equally hair-raising and potentially tragic? He had led a hard life and he was a hard man, yet there was kindness in him and humor and sensitivity. . . . She was finding it hard to concentrate through the haze of pain surrounding her. "I'm so sorry," she whispered.

He glanced up in surprise. "Why?"

He actually didn't know, she realized.

When he went through a hellish experience he just tried to make himself better prepared for the next one. It was a way of life to him. "The pain and the sadness and . . ." She shook her head helplessly. "I'm just sorry."

Daniel's throat tightened. She was the one who was hurting and still she was worrying about him. He touched her cheek with one gentle finger. "Are you?" he asked softly. "Don't be. I survived it." His finger moved down to trace her upper lip. "Did I ever tell you I love to see you smile? It reminds me of warmth and summer and all the good things of life. I haven't seen you laugh yet, but I'm looking forward to it." He bent forward to brush her temple with his lips. "I survived and you're going to survive too, Zilah. Count on it."

"What are you doing?" she asked as he slung the canteen and the M-1 on one shoulder and reached down to gather her in his arms.

"It's generally called a fireman's carry," he said as he slung her facedown over his shoulder. "I want to move fast and this is the easiest way for me to carry you over the kind of terrain we'll be crossing. I'll have to leave the backpack behind. Once we're out of the foothills I'll try to switch your position so that you'll be more comfortable."

"But you can't carry me all that distance," she protested. "Let me try to walk."

He gave her derriere a little slap. "Hush! I can do anything I damn well want to do. It's my decision, and we've already agreed that I'm not a team player. If I let you walk, that poison is going to pour into your bloodstream. Now, be quiet and think good thoughts. That's as far as you're going to be allowed to participate in this little project."

"I think we're going to need all the good thoughts we can beg, borrow, or steal," Zilah murmured hazily. "And even that may not be enough."

"It will be enough." Daniel's voice was grim. "I'll make damn sure it's enough."

"I hope that you . . ." Whatever she had been about to say drifted away as consciousness fled.

Turquoise eyes. They shone cool and glittering in the dark hard face of the stranger. Cool. Zilah's gaze clung to them with desperation. The world was on fire but here was coolness. His voice was cool as well and tinged with dry amusement. "Really, Daniel, I realize the woman is ill but did you have to react so violently? My overseer objected most volubly to being shot at."

"I wasn't shooting at him," Daniel said

grimly. She was being carried down an interminably long hall of mosaic tile, passing white-fretted windows whose intermittent glare hurt her eyes. "He wouldn't have been able to object at all if I had been. I just shattered the exterior mirror on his jeep. The stupid bastard wasn't going to stop when I hailed him down."

"Well, you must admit you do look a bit of a wild man at the moment. Abdul isn't the most courageous man under the best of circumstances. He probably thought you were a bandit."

"Bandits aren't usually wandering around the countryside burdened with an unconscious woman," Daniel growled. "The man is a fool."

"Perhaps," the man with the turquoise eyes drawled. "But he's an excellent overseer. One can't have everything."

"Don't try to give me that bull, Philip," Daniel said. "You know damn well that you'll have everything your own way or blow up the whole world trying."

"I do find life far more convenient that way." Zilah saw again the flint of those turquoise eyes as he glanced down at her dispassionately. "Your Miss Dabala seems quite ill. Was she shot in the escape?"

"Scorpion sting," Daniel said tersely.

106

"She's been in intense pain and drifting in and out of consciousness for the last few hours. She's burning up with fever. As soon as I can get her to bed I want a doctor to see her."

"I've already sent for him. I told Raoul to phone for Dr. Madchen when he informed me that you'd roared into my courtyard with an unconscious woman in the jeep. He should be here shortly."

"She'll need antivenom."

"We keep some here in the first aid room. I'll have Raoul check to be sure it's still fresh. If not, I'll send a courier to pick up some at Dr. Madchen's dispensary."

"Good." She was being placed on a bed whose cool, silken sheets felt like a blessed balm to her hot flesh. Daniel's eyes were narrowed in concern on her face. "Hold on, Zilah, we've almost got it made."

Zilah tried to smile but it hurt too much. Everything hurt too much. She closed her eyes wearily to block out the light that was burning her eyes. She heard Daniel mutter something violent beneath his breath. She paid no attention to it. She had gotten accustomed to that fierce murmur beneath her ear in the last few hours. Now it brought only a feeling of comfort and protection like the growl of a grizzly to her cub.

"You called her Miss Dabala and mentioned the escape," Daniel was saying somewhere above her head in the darkness. "Who told you about Zilah?"

"Your old friend Clancy Donahue became concerned when you failed to contact him last night as arranged. He flew in to be on the spot in case you needed him. He filled me in on the details of your little adventure. It sounded quite entertaining. Just the sort of thing that would amuse you."

"Oh, yes, very amusing," Daniel said caustically. "Next time I must remember to invite you along for the ride." She felt Daniel's hands unbuttoning the collar of her shirt. Strange that she recognized that touch even with her eyes closed. "Where the hell is that doctor?"

"Patience isn't one of your major virtues, Daniel. It's been less than ten minutes since I called him."

"And it's been over two hours since the scorpion stung her. She should have had an antidote at once."

"The doctor's right behind me. I ran into him in the foyer." It was a new voice, deep, authoritative, and vaguely familiar. "He stopped to place a phone call to Karim Ben Raschid's palace to check on her medical history with Zilah's mother when I informed them her records would be there. How is she? I told you to get her out, not get her shot, Daniel."

"Dammit, Clancy, I did get her out," Daniel said harshly. "It was a scorpion, not a bullet. Now, get that doctor in here, or I'll do it myself with a hell of a lot less diplomacy."

Clancy. It must be Clancy Donahue. He had been very kind to her in the past and she wanted to open her eyes and greet him. Yet when she did she could make out only three surreal figures standing before her. Dark, looming, and somehow menacing. Something stirred deep in her memory and started panic coursing wildly through her. Why had she thought she was safe? She was never safe. She would never be safe from them. "Daniel! Daniel!"

One of the shadows bent swiftly. "It's all right, Zilah. I'm here."

"No! Don't touch me. Please don't touch me." Suddenly an agonizing new pain struck her and she clutched at her stomach with a moan.

"What the devil?" The man had Daniel's voice but how did she know they weren't deceiving her again? It had happened before. "What's wrong with her?"

"I would say the venom is causing severe

stomach cramps." Another voice, this one with a slight German accent. "It's not unusual." This shadow was shorter, with a silhouette that was almost rotund. "Your servant informed me that it's a scorpion sting on her right ankle?"

"Don't just stand there looking at her as if she's some kind of bug under a microscope. Get rid of that blasted pain!"

He sounded so concerned. But then, they were always like that, so sleek and smooth, with their soft, mocking voices. She mustn't be fooled into thinking them friends. They didn't care about her pain. It was a weapon they used to make her do what they wanted.

The man with the German accent shrugged. "I was going to give her the anti-venom serum first, but it doesn't matter." He was gone from her vision for a moment and when he returned he was much closer and there was something in his hand. The needle, shining and deadly and evil. *The needle!*

She screamed.

She scrambled to her knees. Dear heaven, she was so weak. They must have given her something before that she didn't remember. Sometimes she didn't remember. She could feel the headboard pressing into her back as she cowered like an animal. "No! I don't want it. Please!"

"Zilah, for God's sake. It's only morphine," the man who was pretending to be Daniel said. "It will take away the pain."

She shook her head wildly. "No shots! I won't let you. It's bad. It's all bad. You're going to let them hurt me again."

"Oh, my God," Clancy breathed. "My God!"

But it wasn't Clancy. She had to remember that. He was one of them.

"Is that all you've got to say?" Daniel's voice was shaking. "I can't take this. Why the hell is she so frightened of us?"

"She's remembering that other time," Clancy answered hoarsely. "And I'm not standing up so well under it myself."

"You will have to hold her," Dr. Madchen said briskly. "She's delirious and will fight the needle. I might hurt her."

"I'll hold her." Turquoise eyes. "Daniel, you hold her other arm."

They closed on her with lightning swiftness and she was helpless. She struggled wildly, panting with fear. "No, don't hurt me. I won't do it. Let me go." The tears were pouring down her cheeks. "Why are you doing this to me? I want to go home."

"Shh. It's all right." Daniel's voice was broken. "No one's going to hurt you. Will

111

you give her the shot, dammit?"

The familiar hot pain in her arm. It was happening again. Despair welled up in her. She stopped struggling. Then the needle was gone and she felt the soft, swooping mist begin to enfold her. The tears continued to rain down her cheeks and she made no attempt to halt them.

Daniel's expression clearly revealed his agonized concern for her. How had they managed to find someone who looked so much like Daniel? For it couldn't have been Daniel. He wouldn't have betrayed her like this. He was easing her stiff body into a reclining position on the bed and releasing her arms. He knew she wouldn't be able to fight him now. They always knew.

"Please. Stop crying. It's tearing me apart."

She shook her head slowly. She closed her eyes so that she could no longer see the face of betrayal. "I just want to go home," she whispered. "Please let me go home."

Her breathing became deep and even. "She's unconscious," Dr. Madchen said. "I'll give her the serum now." He raised a brow at Daniel. "With your permission."

Daniel nodded jerkily. "Give it to her. Is she going to be all right?"

"You've scarcely given me a chance to

112

examine her," Dr. Madchen said caustically as he prepared the syringe. "How would I know?"

Daniel took a step closer, his hand flashing out and closing on the man's throat. "I'm not in the mood for sarcasm at the moment," he said with menacing softness. "I'll ask you again. Is she going to be all right?"

Dr. Madchen's lips tightened. "I see no reason why she shouldn't. There are very few deaths these days from scorpion stings. She should be a bit weak for a few days. However, *if* I'm allowed to treat her, she should recover in a short time."

Philip El Kabbar was frowning. "Let him go, Daniel. I apologize, Dr. Madchen. Daniel is terribly upset at the moment." His blue-green eyes were suddenly twinkling. "Though I suppose you should be grateful he didn't shoot at you as he did at Abdul. He has a tendency to become a bit violent on occasion."

Daniel's hand slowly released the doctor's throat. He stepped back. "You might keep that in mind while you're taking care of her. I want her well." His eyes were blazing fiercely in his white face. "Do you hear me? I want her *well*."

"Then leave the room and let me do my

job." Dr. Madchen turned away. "I would appreciate it if you would get this man out of my way, Sheikh El Kabbar. I don't work well under intimidation."

"Daniel." Clancy's tone was surprisingly gentle. "Come on. You need a drink. She'll be better off without you prowling around getting in the doctor's way." His lips curved in a slightly rueful smile. "I think I could use one myself. I wasn't expecting this to be quite so grueling."

"Grueling." Daniel's nostrils flared. "Hell yes, it was grueling. I feel as if I've been put through a meat grinder. Why the hell would she react like that? She should know that I would never hurt her." His hands clenched at his sides. "My God, she should *know* that."

"She was delirious," Philip said. "Surely that was reason enough."

Daniel shook his head. "There's more to it than that." His gaze narrowed on Clancy. "And I think you know what was going on in her head all that time."

"I'm afraid I do," Clancy said wearily. "I wish to God I didn't. It makes me a little sick."

Daniel turned away abruptly. "We need to talk," he said tersely. "I think a drink would be an excellent idea." He was striding toward the door. He glanced back over his shoulder. "Philip?"

Philip El Kabbar shook his head. "I'll join you later." His sudden smile lent a rare warmth to his dark, cynical face. "I'll watch over your little charge, Daniel. I won't permit anything to happen to her."

"I know you won't," Daniel said gruffly. "We'll be in the study."

Clancy's lips pursed in a low whistle as he strolled beside Daniel down the hall. "I never thought I'd see a ferocious panther like El Kabbar meekly playing nursemaid."

"I've heard the big cats make magnificent guardians for their young," Daniel said. "And Philip isn't all panther. He's been a good friend to me."

"Like to like," Clancy suggested dryly. "Neither one of you can be termed exactly tame."

"And neither can you." Daniel threw open the intricately carved double doors of the study. "Or you wouldn't be in the business you're in. You ought to understand Philip very well."

Clancy shrugged as he watched Daniel cross the room to the small cellarette, his dusty boots sinking into the exquisite Persian carpet. "I understand that side of him well enough. I'm just a little wary of all

115

that power he wields. He could be a very dangerous enemy for Alex to have to deal with if he chose to exert it."

"He won't choose," Daniel said. "As long as Alex doesn't interfere with Philip's territorial rights, he has nothing to worry about." He reached for the cut glass decanter in the cellarette. "Bourbon?"

Clancy nodded. "He wasn't pleased to see me last night. He was even less pleased when I told him about your mission. You're right. He's very protective of those he cares about. I'll have to remember that."

"That's right, file it away in the computer bank you call a memory." Daniel had poured his own brandy and was coming back to stand before Clancy. He handed him the bourbon. "And while you're at it, make a note that there's no way I'll let you use me to hurt him, Clancy." His gaze met Clancy's steadily. "I let you use me this time, but not again." He took a long swallow of his brandy. "Have you heard anything of Hassan and his boys?"

"No sign of them yet." Clancy frowned. "Did you have to blow up the plane?"

"It was the simplest way to get them to follow me into Sedikhan."

"And did they?"

Daniel nodded grimly. "I made sure they'd

116

be mad enough to follow us to hell and back. They'll surface soon. You can bet on it. You just be on the spot to grab them when they do. I don't want them to get near Zilah again. That's why I chose Philip's compound rather than my own — his security is far better than mine."

"How did you manage to —"

"I'll give you a full report later," Daniel interrupted. "Right now, I want some answers myself." He gestured to the high-backed leather chair in front of the Sheraton desk. "You might as well make yourself comfortable. You're not leaving here until I find out what you know."

"Why don't you sit down yourself," Clancy suggested as he dropped down into the chair and stretched his legs out in front of him. "You look like you need a bed, not a chair. Was it a rough caper?"

"We've both been through worse." Daniel made a face as he looked down at his dust-grimed khakis and the sweat-darkened undershirt clinging to his chest. "And I don't think Philip would appreciate my lolling in his antique chairs in my present condition." He half sat, half leaned against the edge of the desk. "I can rest later. Talk to me."

"Zilah?"

"Who else?" Daniel's hand tightened on his glass. "You know why she looked at me as if I were her executioner."

Clancy lowered his gaze to the amber liquid in his glass. "I told you I wasn't at liberty to discuss Zilah with strangers. David would have my head in a handbasket if I did."

"Dammit, I'm not a stranger," Daniel burst out with savage violence. "Can't you see that I *need* to know?"

"Yes, I think I can see that," Clancy said thoughtfully. "Experiences like what the two of you have shared together have a way of melding two people together, but it's something more than that, isn't it?"

Daniel inhaled raggedly. "It's something more," he said tightly. "I'm not asking to know anything about her relationship with Bradford. I just need to know what made her look at me the way she did." The pain of that moment was still like a raw wound within him. It had been doubled because he had felt the pain and despair in Zilah as if it were his own.

"But her relationship with David is part of what you saw in that bedroom this morning. You can't separate the two." Clancy shook his head. "You're not going to like it. It's not going to be comfortable to live with.

Not if you care for her."

"Tell me."

"When she was thirteen years old Zilah was living with her grandmother in Marasef while her mother acted as housekeeper for Karim Ben Raschid. She was a bright, pretty little girl, always bubbling with enthusiasm and laughter. One day she disappeared. She just never came home from school. Her mother was frantic. She went to the police, searched the streets herself, and did everything she could think of doing. Then she asked David Bradford to help. Six months had passed by that time and the trail was cold, but he and Alex finally located her." He paused. "She was in a bordello called the House of the Yellow Door. She had been taken by a vice ring that specialized in kidnapping young girls, drugging them with heroin until they were hopelessly addicted, and using them as prostitutes." He ignored the exclamation Daniel made. "I don't have to tell you what kind of shape she was in when David brought her back to Zalandan. It took her almost eight months to lick the heroin addiction." His lips curved in a bitter smile. "After that there was only the psychological damage of the experience itself to contend with. A real piece of cake."

Thirteen," Daniel said jerkily. "She was

just a child." He covered his eyes with his hand. "My God, I feel sick."

"David sent her to live with his parents in Texas and she hasn't been back to Sedikhan until now. She's been under psychiatric care all these years and has made a remarkable recovery." He frowned. "But judging from what I saw today, it obviously wasn't a total recovery."

"How the hell could it be?" Daniel's voice was muffled. "I don't know how she even survived it."

"She survived it because she's an exceptionally strong personality," Clancy said. "It was her choice to come back to Sedikhan for this visit. She thought she could handle it."

"She thinks she can handle everything in the whole damn world."

"Does she?" A slight smile touched Clancy's lips. "That's good to know." He took a sip of his bourbon. "So there's the story. Is there anything else you want to know?"

"Just one thing." Daniel's hand dropped from his face, revealing eyes that were cold as death. "Did you get rid of them?"

Clancy nodded. "The vice ring was smashed and the head of it was taken care of in a very permanent manner."

"I almost wish he hadn't been," Daniel

said tautly. "I need to kill him. I need to do something to help her." He closed his eyes. "I feel so damned helpless, I think I'm going to explode."

There was a flicker of sympathy in Clancy's hard face. "We all felt the same way when it happened. You were lucky not to have been around to see her right after we found her. It was enough to tear your heart out."

"I don't think I was lucky. Bradford was there to help her and I wasn't," Daniel said harshly. "If I had been there, she would never have looked at me as if I were some kind of monster. She would have known she could trust me."

"She was burning up with fever. She didn't know what was happening. She obviously thought she was back in that bordello."

"Oh, yes, I realize all that." Daniel's mirthless laugh had a touch of desperation in it. "I also realize that after an experience like that she's going to have a hell of a time trusting or responding to any man." Dear Lord, that was putting it mildly. He had been so confident last night that he could ease friendship into a commitment. He had been almost brutal when he had taken Zilah. It was a wonder that she hadn't run away from him screaming instead of yielding so sweetly. She couldn't have enjoyed it. Gratitude or pity? It didn't matter. He just hoped he hadn't done any permanent damage by lovemaking that must have appeared closer to rape to Zilah. He had to make sure that she knew it wouldn't always be like that. That he was capable of treating her with the gentleness and care her fragility demanded.

"Surely you aren't thinking about getting involved with her?" Clancy asked. "May I point out that you've known the woman only one day?"

"I'm already involved." Daniel tossed the rest of his brandy down his throat and set his glass on the desk with barely restrained violence. "I didn't ask for it, but there it is. She's mine now, problems or no problems."

Clancy stiffened. "I hope you're not speaking in the carnal sense. According to the last psychiatrist's report Zilah still isn't able to respond sexually to any man. I sure as hell didn't send you out there to seduce the girl. I'm not sure David would tolerate that kind of action on your part."

"God!" Daniel's stomach muscles clenched as if someone had knocked the breath out of him. It was even worse than he had imagined. She was still scarred, still hurting, and he hadn't even been particularly gentle with her in the first experience she'd had since that nightmare. Yet she had responded. At least he had thought she had responded at the time. How could he be sure with the swirling darkness and the earthquake of passion that had shaken him? Perhaps she had only submitted. Dear heaven, he hoped that hadn't been the case. If it was, then it was no wonder she had mistaken him for one of those monsters from her childhood.

He was trembling, he realized with disgust. This wasn't the time to give in to weakness. He still had Clancy to deal with, and that was never easy. "Too damn bad," Daniel said coolly. "You can tell Bradford she's no longer his concern."

"And what about Zilah? Doesn't she have any say in this?"

"Do you think I'm going to lock her in a room and rape her?" Daniel's expression was a mask of pain. "She's never going to know fear or pain again as long as she lives. I'll see to that. But I'm not letting her go, Clancy. I can't run the risk of her shying away from me as she did this afternoon. Evidently it wouldn't take much to trigger that panic again. That rules out any type of normal courtship."

"What are you suggesting then?"

"I'm not suggesting anything, Clancy," Daniel said quietly. "I'm telling you I need time and that you're going to get it for me."

"Time?"

Daniel nodded. "Zilah stays here for two weeks alone with me. I don't want any interference from Bradford or her mother or anyone else. Not even you, Clancy. I'm going to have enough problems without trying to fight my way through a battery of protective guardians."

"You're out of line, Daniel," Clancy said crisply. "You know I can't arrange that."

"I know you're going to have to do your damnedest," Daniel said with a cool little smile. "Or else you're going to have to face just the awkward diplomatic confrontation you've been trying to avoid between Alex and Philip."

Clancy's eyes narrowed to ice blue slits. "You'd bring El Kabbar into it?"

"If I have to," Daniel said. "That's up to you. You know Philip wouldn't bat an eye to closing his borders and refusing to let Zilah leave or anyone to come in after her. He'd probably enjoy testing his power against the Ben Raschid regime."

"I wouldn't doubt that for a minute," Clancy growled. "Dammit, Daniel, I won't be manipulated this way. You're bluffing."

"Then call my bluff." Daniel's eyes were gleaming recklessly. "And take the consequences. Or give me my two weeks and then I'll bring her to Zalandan myself." He paused. "If she still wants to go."

"And just how do you propose I accomplish this hiatus?" Clancy's tone was heavy with sarcasm.

"That's up to you. We both know you have guile to spare when you choose to exert it. If it will help, I'll get Philip to have the doctor issue orders that she's not to be moved for that length of time."

"And I only have to keep the homefront from finding out she's being held by a man who'd like nothing better than to tumble Zilah into his bed. Considering her circumstances, that particular knowledge would alarm the hell out of everyone." Clancy scowled. "I don't suppose you'd like to give me your assurance that that won't happen?"

Daniel shook his head. "I want her more than I've ever wanted any woman before, so I can't promise anything." His expression was grim. "But I want her trust as well. That means I can't have both. Not right now."

"Well, that's something at least." Clancy stood up. "You have your two weeks. You leave me very little choice." He placed his glass on the desk with careful precision. "I don't like to be put in that position," he said softly. "Remember that, Daniel. You're walking on thin ice."

"I know." Daniel grinned suddenly. "That should prove how serious I am about this. You always did scare the hell out of me, Clancy."

A reluctant smile tugged at Clancy's lips. He uttered an obscenity that was explicit. "Two weeks. After that I'm coming in to get her and to hell with diplomacy." His smile took on a silky ferocity. "And I'll nail your ass to the wall of the Tower of Tears at Marasef."

"We'll see." Daniel slanted an engimatic smile at him as he straightened. "You've only played the game *with* me, Clancy. Never against me. You might be in for a surprise. Now that we've reached an agreement, I want to get back to Zilah." He strode briskly toward the door. "Let me know if you get any word on Hassan."

"Daniel."

Daniel looked back over his shoulder inquiringly.

"This must mean a hell of a lot to you," Clancy said slowly. "But are you sure it's worth the possibility of having to go up against Alex?"

"It's worth it." Daniel's smile was bittersweet. "I feel as if I've found something I've been searching for all my life. I should have known it wouldn't come without a barb or two attached." He opened the door. "But, hell yes, it's worth it."

When Zilah opened her eyes, she saw Daniel. It was obviously night, for it was dark in the room, but there was a lamp burning on the bedside table and Daniel was sitting in a wing chair drawn close to the side of the bed. There was a frown on his face as he gazed abstractedly into the distance.

"Daniel?" she murmured drowsily to bring him back to her. She shifted in the bed, turning to face him. She was naked beneath the satin sheet that covered her, she noticed absently.

He straightened and leaned forward. "I'm here. Go back to sleep, babe. You're safe now."

"I know." She was always safe with Daniel. "Are you all right?"

"I'm fine and you will be too. Dr. Madchen said that you'd be weak and lethargic for a few days, but after that you'll be on the mend."

"Dr. Madchen?"

He went still. "You don't remember the

doctor?"

She shook her head. "It's all pretty much of a blur. I remember you carrying me into a foyer that looked like something out of an Arabian Nights palace. After that, it was all downhill." She frowned. "No, I remember something else."

There was a flicker of wariness in Daniel's eyes. "Really?"

"A man with strange-colored eyes. Almost turquoise. Was that the doctor?"

Daniel chuckled. "No, that was your host, Philip El Kabbar. He'll be flattered to know that he made such an impression even while you were in the throes of fever. It will give his ego an enormous boost. Not that he needs it."

"It's very kind of him to let us impose on him like this. I'd like to thank him."

"You'll get plenty of opportunity to do that." Daniel reached out and took her hand in his. "The doctor doesn't want you traveling on to Zalandan for a week or so. He wants to be sure you don't develop complications."

Her eyes widened. "Why should he think I'd have complications?"

He looked down at her hand and idly began to stroke the pulse point at her wrist with his thumb. "Complications have a habit of popping up when you least expect them," he said evasively. "We're going to be very careful of you, Zilah." He glanced up, his eyes twinkling. "After all the trouble I took to get you away from Hassan, I refuse to lose you to a scorpion."

His gentle massaging thumb was sending sparks of heat up her arm, and Zilah felt a tiny sensuous stirring in the pit of her stomach. "I wouldn't think of having all your efforts in my behalf come to nothing," she said lightly. "It would be most ungrateful of me." She couldn't seem to pull her gaze away from its entanglement with Daniel's. "I'll be dutiful in making a complete recovery. Has anyone notified my mother and David that I'm safe?"

"We phoned Zalandan as soon as the doctor said you were out of danger. Clancy Donahue flew back there tonight and will give them a more personal report. You'll be able to phone your mother tomorrow yourself if you like."

"Of course." Her forehead wrinkled in a frown. "Clancy Donahue was here too? The fever must have really caused me to draw a blank. What else did I miss?"

"Nothing of importance." He gave her hand an affectionate squeeze before releasing it. "Do you think you can go back to sleep now that you've had some of your questions answered?"

"But I don't have all my questions answered." She was scanning his face with a troubled expression. There were lines of strain around Daniel's eyes and the flesh was drawn taut over his cheekbones. "Haven't you slept at all?"

He chuckled. "I don't need much sleep. I was fine after I showered and had something to eat."

"I don't think you slept last night either. And I don't see how you possibly could have slept the night before, planting all those bombs and whatevers."

He grinned. "Yes, planting whatevers can be very exhausting."

"Don't joke. You know perfectly well what I mean. Go to bed, Daniel."

"Now, if you'd said *come* instead of *go,* I might be more amiable about the suggestion," Daniel drawled.

She felt the heat in her stomach flutter and then begin to spread. "Then, come," she said breathlessly.

The smile was abruptly gone from his face. He had a sudden heated memory of her nails digging into his hips while she murmured the word that had broken his restraint into a million pieces. "You mean it?"

"We've slept together before." She moistened her lips nervously. "You need the rest."

The flame that had leaped fitfully in his eyes disappeared suddenly. "I appreciate your concern, but the situation is a little different now."

Zilah glanced around the luxurious room, with its gleaming mosaic-tiled floors covered with richly patterned area rugs. "Externally, perhaps." Her eyes met his uncertainly. "But we're the same people we were last night in that cave, aren't we?"

He stood up. "We're still the same people." He smiled gently. "Clancy said that danger had a way of bringing two people close in a hurry. I think he's right. I couldn't feel closer to you, old friend."

Old friend. Last night when he had murmured that phrase in her ear it had brought her only warm contentment. Now, for some reason, it made her feel a little uneasy. She was probably just being stupidly imaginative to think there was an odd tension in Daniel's attitude. "I feel very close to you too, Daniel," she said softly. "And very grateful."

His eyes, which had been carefully guarded, suddenly flared to life. "I thought

we'd already discussed how I regard gratitude. You can save that for Bradford. I'll
have none of it." Then, when he saw the
startled confusion in her expression, he took
a deep breath and tried to smile re-
assuringly. "Sorry. You should know by now
what a rough bastard I am. Maybe you're
right about my being tired. Forget it. Okay?"

"Okay," she said, still puzzled.

"That's my girl." He tousled her hair affectionately. "You go back to sleep. I promise
I'll work at being halfway civilized the next
time I see you."

"Don't work too hard. I like you pretty
well just the way you are." Her eyes were
wide and uncertain, looking up at him. "You
will be here when I wake up, won't you?"
She smiled shakily. "I mean, you don't have
any other terrorists to catch or planes to
blow up or anything?"

"I'll be here." He kept his tone deliberately
offhand. "I thought I'd stick around until
you were well and then escort you to Zalandan myself. After all, you're still technically
my responsibility. I always like to tie up all
the loose ends on any mission I undertake."

She felt a little ripple of pain mixing with
the joy that news brought her. Responsibility. She was sure he hadn't meant to hurt
her. He couldn't know just how bone-weary

she was of being a responsibility to every-one. She smiled with an effort. "That sounds like fun. It will be interesting to see what kind of pyrotechnics you can instigate on a more conventional journey."

He bent forward and brushed a fairy-light kiss on her forehead. "I'll try to see what I can do to keep you amused." He straight-ened and reached for the switch on the lamp. He suddenly hesitated. "Would you rather I left the light on?"

"Why should I?" she asked curiously. "I'm not a child afraid of the dark."

"No, of course you're not. I guess I wasn't thinking straight." The light flicked off, plunging the room into darkness. "Good night, Zilah."

"Good night, Daniel." She felt bereft as she watched his massive shadow stride toward the door on the far side of the room. "Daniel?"

He paused as he opened the door. The dim light from the hall haloed his auburn head with flame, but left the rest of him in silhouette. "Yes?"

"I have one more question. Who un-dressed me?"

There was a short silence before he an-swered. "I did. I undressed you and bathed you myself. Philip has no women servants. I thought you'd rather have me do it than a stranger."

She felt a sultry tingle of awareness sweep through her. Good heavens, she was supposed to be ill and yet even the thought of Daniel's hands and eyes on her naked body sent a wrenching stab of desire for him through her. From frigidity to nymphomania in one experience, she thought ruefully. No, not nymphomania. It was only Daniel that she wanted. Only Daniel. "You were right," she said huskily. "Thank you."

"You're welcome." He hesitated, and when he spoke again the words came jerkily. "You're a very beautiful woman, Zilah. A very special woman. I hope . . ." His words trailed off. "Good night." The door closed softly behind him.

There was a tiny frown creasing Zilah's forehead as she turned on her side and settled her cheek on the satin pillow. Her uneasiness was growing by the minute. Why had Daniel been so reserved, almost cool with her? It couldn't have been entirely her imagination. In the brief time they had known each other she had learned to read him too well to mistake the signs of his withdrawal.

Perhaps he was having second thoughts about the so-called obsession he had formed for her. The thought sent a chill of depression through her and she drew the sheet up to her chin with a little shiver. Well, what if he had? He was probably right to be wary of a relationship that had started so precipitously and had exploded with such wild force. Perhaps he had satisfied his desire for her and no longer wanted her in that way anymore. What did she know about how long it took for men to tire of women? She should be equally sensible and offer Daniel the platonic friendship he appeared to want now. She knew that friendship lasted. *If* that was what he wanted. Oh, she just didn't know. Last night everything had seemed so beautifully certain and now she was miserably unsure.

Then she determinedly cleared her mind of doubts and closed her eyes. The man was completely exhausted. She was foolish to try to analyze his actions when she couldn't possibly expect him to behave in a normal manner. For that matter, how did she know what his normal behavior was? They still had to get to know the more obscure facets of each other's personalities. All that would come in time. She wasn't going to lose the precious gift Daniel had given her. Not now that she knew what they could have together. It would hurt too much. She didn't think she would be able to stand it.

What was she thinking? Of course she would be able to stand it. She was strong. She could stand anything. She closed her eyes and tried to let the serenity of that knowledge flow into her. It surrounded her, whirling doubts and fear away, but beneath it was a barely discernible chorus that sang her a wistful siren's song.

I will be strong. I will survive. But, please, just this one time, let me not have to use that strength. Let me have Daniel. Please. Let me have Daniel.

5

Turquoise eyes gazed down at her. Zilah opened her own eyes with a distinct sense of déjà vu as she looked up in drowsy bewilderment into the face of the man standing by her bed.

"I'm Philip El Kabbar, Miss Dabala. I apologize for barging in on you so unceremoniously. I wished to welcome you to my home, and assure you that if there's anything you need or want, you have only to ask." His smile was charming. "I would have waited, but I had to leave early to go to the irrigation project and I wanted to be sure to see you before I left. I hope you will forgive me?"

There wouldn't be many women who would fail to forgive Philip El Kabbar almost any transgression, Zilah thought as she sat up in bed, tucking the satin sheet firmly beneath her arms. He was one of the most fantastically attractive men she had ever seen. He was in his early thirties, she concluded, with raven-dark hair and skin bronzed to a dark gold, high, hollowed cheekbones and a well-shaped mouth that held a hint of leashed sexuality. Leashed. Yes, everything about him fit that word. His tall, slim frame, garbed in casual blue jeans and a black sweatshirt, gave the impression of tremendous strength, rigidly restrained. His expression was a smooth, guarded mask of charm. Those striking blue-green eyes were cool and slightly cynical beneath slashing dark brows.

"I should be the one to apologize for intruding into your household, Sheikh El Kabbar," she said. "You've been very kind. I promise I won't abuse your hospitality any longer than I have to."

He shrugged. "Daniel wishes you to remain here. My home has many rooms and the servants have little to do. You are welcome to stay as long as Daniel enjoys your presence."

Well, that certainly put her firmly in her place, she thought wryly. It appeared that the sheikh's charming façade was just that. Beneath that mask was an almost brutal honesty and a touch of ruthlessness. "It's not a question of my entertainment value, Sheikh El Kabbar," she said dryly. "When my health is improved, I'll leave with or without Daniel. I'm not a harem girl or khadim waiting on any man's pleasure. In case you haven't heard, Sedikhan has outlawed slavery in any form."

"But the laws of Sedikhan don't necessarily apply to my province," he said with a slight smile. "I believe you'll find that out shortly. I run my lands to suit myself." His gaze raked slowly over her. "You're a very lovely woman. I can see how Daniel would be intrigued by you. If you are generous with your body, he will treat you well. He is kind to his women." His lips twisted. "Far kinder than I. You would be wise to be less defiant and more accommodating. It is, after all, what a woman is most proficient at doing."

She shook her head incredulously. "I can't believe this. You're speaking as if women have no wills or minds of their own."

"Am I?" The slashing black brows lifted mockingly. "I have no desire to give that impression. I know women can have extraordinarily strong wills. As for their mental powers" — he lifted one shoulder in a half shrug — "they can be very cunning as well."

"Cunning?" Zilah echoed distastefully. "What a horribly denigrating word. I regard myself as intelligent, but I am *not* cunning."

She frowned. "Do you always speak to women so insultingly?"

"No, usually I'm quite flowery and utterly charming," he drawled outrageously. "I'm only honest with them when they might offer a threat to me or mine."

Her eyes widened. "You think I'm some kind of a threat?"

"It's a possibility." His eyes were cool, shimmering ice floes. "As I said, Daniel is intrigued. It is not like Daniel to regard women in a serious light. He was very emotional yesterday when you were so ill. Emotion has a way of weakening a man's defenses. I will not have him hurt, Miss Dabala. You must ply your woman's wiles on someone else. Do you understand?"

"Perfectly," she said calmly. "I'm to fall meekly into Daniel's bed, but on no account am I to venture to think or regard myself as anything but a vassal." She lifted a brow. "Have I got it right?"

He nodded. "Perhaps you are more intelligent than cunning after all, Miss Dabala. You're quite correct."

"I just wanted to make sure I understood." She met his eyes and said clearly, "Go to hell, Sheikh El Kabbar."

There was a flicker of surprise in his face, followed by a touch of amusement. "I've found some women capable of sending men there, but not by suggestion alone. I'm afraid you're going to have to do better than that."

"I have no desire to try to influence your destiny in any way, Sheikh El Kabbar," she said wearily. "Or Daniel's either. All I want to do is to get well enough to go to Zalandan. The minute the doctor releases me, I won't bother you again."

"Ah, but the doctor is a very cautious man where certain patients are concerned. You may be with us for some time. That's why I thought we should have this chat." His smile was brilliant in his bronzed face. "Enjoy your stay with us, Miss Dabala. I promise that on the next occasion we meet I'll be as meticulously polite and diplomatic as anyone could wish."

"I'd rather you'd be rude but honest," she said bluntly. "I haven't any use for polite deception."

For an instant there was a trace of admiration in those guarded eyes. "I can see how you would appeal to Daniel. He has a great respect for honesty as well. That was why I was a bit alarmed when —" He broke off. His gaze narrowed thoughtfully on her face. "Respect and admiration are far more dangerous than lust. I'll have to keep a close eye on you, Miss Dabala." His gaze once more traveled over her, lingering on her naked shoulders above the sheet. There was suddenly a fugitive twinkle in his eyes. "A task I'm going to take a good deal of aesthetic pleasure in performing." Before she could reply he had turned away and was strolling toward the door. "You have such superb skin that it's really a shame to cover even an inch of it, but Daniel's being very stuffy about not keeping you totally naked for the duration of your stay here. As your own clothing was blown up with the plane, I've taken the liberty of ordering you a complete wardrobe from the stores in Marasef." He glanced back over his shoulder, his eyes gleaming with mischief. "Don't worry, Daniel also insisted on paying for everything, so you're not beholden to me for a single handkerchief. What a pity. I enjoy having beautiful women in my debt. Good day, Miss Dabala."

Zilah found herself staring at the closed door with a mixture of indignation and amusement. Philip El Kabbar was utterly impossible, obviously a complete male chauvinist and more arrogant than even a ruling sheikh had any right to be. She should be ready to roast him over open flames after that little conversation. Yet there had been a thread of warmth and humor beneath the mask of glittering hardness that for some inexplicable reason had kept her from feeling too much animosity.

There was a perfunctory knock on the door, and it swung open. Daniel entered, balancing a covered rattan tray in one hand and a large box in the other. He was dressed even more casually than El Kabbar had been, in cut off jeans and an army-green tank top. However, nothing about Daniel's vitality was leashed. It was almost an explosive force as he strode into the room. "I ran into Philip in the hall," he said grimly as he kicked the door shut with his sandaled foot and strode toward the bed. "Was he decent to you?"

"Isn't he usually decent to his guests?" she asked evasively.

"Don't play word games with me, Zilah." He tossed the box he was carrying on the bed and settled the tray on her lap. "I want an answer from you." He sat down on the bed beside her and plucked the napkin from the covered tray to reveal eggs and fingers of buttered toast. "Eat your breakfast."

A little smile tugged at her lips. "Which do you want me to do first?"

"Both." He scowled. "Hell, I wanted to be here to run interference for you. I only stopped for a minute to pick up that box from the helicopter. I should have known Philip would do something to upset you."

"He didn't upset me," she said as she took a bite of toast. "I had no trouble holding my own with your friend, the sheikh. Though I think he was doing his best to intimidate me. He appears to have very little respect for the gentler sex."

"That's because he's never found them to be particularly gentle." He too picked up a piece of toast from her plate and began to nibble it absentmindedly. "That, along with having a father who believed all women belonged in a seraglio, wasn't conducive to developing warm and tender feelings toward womankind. He doesn't trust them worth a damn and acts accordingly."

"Is that why he doesn't have any women servants?"

"Probably. I never asked him," he said. "Look, I know he said something that wasn't exactly hospitable. When I told him you were staying for a bit, he had that thoughtful look that usually means trouble. I'd appreciate it if you'd ignore it. Philip is a good friend to me. I'll see that it doesn't happen again."

"He is a good friend to you. That was why he was trying to save you from my vampish ways. I got the distinct impression he believed I was about to clip all your locks off as Delilah did Samson's." She tilted her head to look at him with mock objectivity. "I could have told him that with your beard it would be entirely too much trouble."

Daniel's hand rose quickly to his jaw. "You don't like my beard?"

She had a fleeting memory of the soft virile brush of that beard rubbing against her naked breasts and she felt a sudden thrust of aching heat go through her. She dropped her eyes to her plate. "I like it. I just don't have any desire to wear it on my belt as a trophy." She smiled. "That particular shade of red doesn't go well with my coloring."

"Oh, I don't know," he said blandly. "I think you could get used to wearing me on your person in no time at all." He took another bite of toast before adding softly, "Or in your person."

Her startled gaze flew up to meet his. His eyes were soft and midnight-dark and his face was filled with sensuality. She was abruptly conscious of the warm hardness of his naked thigh pressing against her own through the thin satin barrier of the sheet. There was a sudden tingling clenching between her thighs that made her inhale sharply.

Daniel muttered a curse beneath his breath and got to his feet. "Dammit, I told you I was a roughneck. Things just come out." He ran his fingers through his hair. "I'll try to watch it."

Why was Daniel upset? The remark hadn't been obscene, merely suggestive. Yet Daniel was acting as if he'd just propositioned a nun. "It didn't offend me," she said, bewildered.

"Good," he said briskly. He bent over the bed and opened the lid of a large box he'd brought into the room just before he'd gotten her breakfast tray. "These are for you. There are more boxes in the helicopter. The servants will bring them in later. I went through this one and it seems to contain all you'll need for right now." He pulled out wisps of lacy underthings and a chocolate-colored robe that was only a sheer float of accordion pleats. "I suppose I should have expected something like this. Philip ordered the wardrobe from the same store his khadims usually use."

"Considering his attitude toward women, it doesn't really surprise me," Zilah said dryly. "He probably thinks that's our sole role in life and we should dress for it. I can't

146

say I'm overly fond of your friend."

"That bad, was he?" Daniel asked gloomily. "I was afraid he might be. Well, you may not be crazy about his manners, but he has one attribute that will win your approval."

"And what is that?"

"He's a damn fine rider and has one of the most famous stables in the Middle East. I'll take you to see it tomorrow if you're well enough."

Zilah's face lit up. "Horses? I'd love to see them. Couldn't we go today? I feel fine."

Daniel was shaking his head. "Not today. You may feel fit, but you're bound to have a reaction from the fever you had yesterday. The doctor said you were to take it easy for the next few days. That means today you stay in bed."

Zilah's expression clouded mutinously. "But I feel fine. I'm very tough usually. I don't know why that scorpion sting affected me so violently."

"You may think you're Annie Oakley and Calamity Jane rolled into one, but today you're definitely playing Camille." He turned to the door. "Finish your breakfast. I'll go to the study and see if I can find a few games to keep you occupied. Any preferences?"

"I want to see the horses," she said stubbornly. "I wouldn't try to ride them without the sheikh's permission, of course. I just want to see them."

"Games," Daniel repeated firmly as he strode through the doorway. "I'll be back in a few minutes to pick up the tray. Eat."

He was doing it again. Just because she'd been so helpless after she'd been stung by the scorpion, he was taking charge and giving orders as if she had no will or mind of her own. She lifted the tray off her lap and set it on the bed beside her. She'd had enough to eat, blast it. She'd also had enough orders for one day. First, El Kabbar with his autocratic instructions, and now Daniel. She wasn't about to lie in bed and be waited on by Daniel. He had already done too much for her. When he came back she would tell him that, but she had better look less like the Camille of Daniel's metaphor when she did it. The first thing she needed was a shower and then to brush her teeth and wash her hair. . . .

She was already tossing the sheet aside and swinging her legs to the floor as she reached for the dark brown negligee. It was just as transparent as she had feared, and she made a face as she slipped into its sheer folds and buttoned the top button. She gathered up the bra and panties, her eyes on the intricately carved door across the room that must lead to the bathroom. Her legs were shaky and her right ankle throbbed in protest as she got slowly to her feet. She would be all right in a moment, she assured herself staunchly. Her head was swimming, but that was probably perfectly natural after being in bed almost twenty-four hours. She took a deep breath and some of the dizziness subsided.

All she had to do was to take it slowly and she'd be fine. She took another step forward and then another. Unfortunately, the philosophy of mind over matter seemed not to be working in this case. Her knees were now shaking so badly that by the time she got halfway across the room she could scarcely control them. It took only a slight stumble on the edge of the Persian carpet to send her tumbling in a heap on the floor.

"Damn!" She could feel the helpless tears mist her eyes and she blinked them back determinedly. So stupid to be upset over a little tumble. It must be because she was so wretchedly weak. She had struggled to her knees and was about to try to get to her feet again when the door swung open.

"Good Lord in heaven!" Daniel exploded. He slammed the door behind him, strode across the room, and tossed the three boxes he was carrying on the bed. "What the hell do you think you're doing? I leave you alone for a few minutes and you're up running around." He was standing before her now and his dark blue eyes were blazing. He grasped her shoulders and hauled her unceremoniously to her feet.

"I just wanted to take a shower," she said defensively. "And brush my teeth."

"And then see the horses," he added grimly. "I wish I had never mentioned them to you."

"I planned that for later," she said with dignity. "I just wanted to be really clean again. I'm a total mess. Just look at me."

"I am," he said huskily. He had been trying to keep from doing just that since the moment he'd walked into the room. She was beautifully, lushly naked beneath the sheer dark brown of the negligee. He could see the dark pink thrust of the nipples that crowned her full breasts, the slim silkiness of her waist and abdomen beneath the material that veiled instead of covered. His gaze was drawn irresistibly to the shadowy triangle at the apex of her thighs, and he felt an aching thrust of desire in his loins. Her sun-burnished hair was falling in shining clouds around her shoulders, and he wanted to reach out and tangle his hand in her locks. To press her close to him so that he could feel that dark, shadowy softness against his hardness.

God, he could almost feel her rubbing against him, her nipples tautening for him as they had in the cave that night. They were peaking now as he looked at her, and he felt a jolt of need so intense it was painful. The bed was so damned close and she *would* want it. She might be frightened at first, but she had been responsive before. Hell, she was responsive now. He could see the pulse pounding wildly in the hollow of her throat and he reached out a hand to half encircle it, pressing his thumb gently to that revealing pulsing. He bent forward, his lips only a breath from hers. He could see the faint cut where Hassan had struck her and he felt a surge of primitive rage rush through him that somehow only intensified the desire he was experiencing. "Is your lip still sore?"

"What?" She had forgotten about it. It was a moment before she could pull her attention from the spell Daniel was weaving about her with only the light touch of his hand and the smoky hotness of his eyes. "Oh, no." She nervously moistened her lips with her tongue. She felt his hand on her throat tighten compulsively. "It doesn't hurt at all anymore."

"That's good," he said hoarsely. He could feel her warmth reaching out to him through the film of material separating them. It would take only a motion of his hand to brush aside the robe and close his fingers on her breast. To lift that rosy nipple to his lips and nibble and suck until she gave that little breathless moan that excited him so. She would dig her fingers into his shoulders as she had in the darkness of the cave. He had noticed in the shower this morning that he still had the marks of her nails on his body. Such a little thing, but it had caused an instant arousal that had forced him to change the flow of water in the shower from warm to ice cold. Then he would run his hands slowly down her smooth warm back. He would cup her buttocks in his palms and lift her, press her against his aching arousal, make her take him into —

Make her take him! The shock of that subconscious thought sent an electrifying jolt through him. He had been within an inch of plunging into her like a rutting stag, not caring whether she wanted it or not. His only concern had been the need for release from the painful aching in his loins. He felt sick with disgust. Only yesterday he had told Clancy that he wasn't going to touch her, that he was going to teach her to trust him. He had been the one who was going to show her that all men weren't animals. His predicament would have been funny if it hadn't possessed the elements of tragedy. Even realizing how close he had come, he was still trembling like a hound who had just scented a bitch in heat. And the most maddening aspect of this entire situation was that he could tell Zilah didn't even realize it existed. It was all there in the clear wonder of the eyes gazing up at him. In spite of her experiences as a child, she still possessed an innocence that amazed him. She knew about violation but she obviously wasn't aware of the more subtle nuances of sexual arousal. The time she had spent in the House of the Yellow Door was a thing apart for her, not connected with their relationship. She was even accepting their lovemaking in the cave as a temporary aberration on his part. Perhaps he should be grateful she was looking at it like that.

His hand fell from her throat to her shoulder and pushed her gently away. What had they been talking about? He could only remember dark pink crests crowning full golden breasts and . . . "You wanted to take a shower?"

A shower? Yes, she definitely needed a shower. She was trembling all over and her knees were weak again, but not from any physical disability. "Yes, I was going to take a shower," she said vaguely.

"We'll see what we can do." He released her shoulders and stepped back. She swayed. He quickly braced her again. "Damn, you can scarcely stand up. How do you expect to take a shower? Hell, you'd probably faint and drown before I could get in to pull you out."

He was angry again. She tried to clear her mind of the sensual mist that was clouding it. Why was he so angry with her when a moment ago he had been so gentle? Now there was no hint of anything but harshness in his face, and she felt a throb of pain tighten her chest. She lifted her chin. "I'll manage. I won't need your help."

"The devil you won't." He cradled her in his left arm and she found herself being half pushed, half carried toward the bathroom door. "Unless you want Philip's valet, Raoul, to help you, I'm the only game in town. Believe me, I don't like the idea any more than you do."

He threw open the door to reveal a bathroom that was the ultimate in sybaritic luxury. A long, mirrored vanity flanked one wall. In a corner, immediately to the left of the door, was a shower stall with frosted glass doors. The center of the room was occupied by a sunken tub that was as large as some swimming pools Zilah had seen. It was tiled in a mosaic rose and ivory floral design, and at the opposite end of the tub were two wide steps leading down into its gleaming depths.

Daniel slammed the door behind them and lifted Zilah onto the vanity before turning to kneel by the gold faucets at the head of the tub. He swiftly turned them on full blast. Clouds of steam swirled around him as he sat back on his haunches, keeping his eyes carefully averted from her and fixed on the gushing water. "This will take only a minute to fill."

"I thought I was going to take a shower."

"A bath is better. I'd have to get into the shower stall with you. It would be a little crowded."

The thought of that intimacy made her throat tighten. "I suppose you're right. I'll be able to manage on my own in the tub."

"The hell you will." He was pouring pink liquid from a small cut crystal flagon that he had snatched from a tray on the side of the tub, and the water exploded into millions of bubbles. "I'll bathe you myself and then I'll know you're all right."

"You're pouring in too much bubble bath."

He continued to tilt the liquid into the already soapy water. "You're wrong there," he said grimly. "There can't be too many bubbles in the world at the moment." He set the empty container on the side of the tub, tested the water to make sure it wasn't too hot, turned off the faucets, and rose lithely to his feet. "Come on, let's get this over with."

He swung her off the vanity, his fingers unbuttoning the top button of her negligee with total impersonality.

Zilah felt a shiver run through her that had nothing to do with her nudity as he stripped the filmy negligee off her and then picked her up. He was so remote, so cold. She had never imagined Daniel could be so cold. "You don't have to bother. Once I'm in the tub I'll be able —"

"Zilah," Daniel said between his teeth. "Shut up!"

Then she was being lowered carefully into the mountains and mountains of soap bubbles. She sneezed. "I knew you were using too much bubble bath. I'm practically drowning in bubbles."

He released her and stood up. He kicked his sandals off as he regarded her appraisingly. It was true. There wasn't an inch of that lovely body visible. She was up to her chin in foam. He felt some of the tension drain out of him. "You look fine to me," he said with a grin. "Kinda cute."

She sneezed again. "Let some of the water out."

"Nope, you'll be in there for only a few minutes." He was settling himself on the first step leading down into the sunken tub. He tossed her a sponge and a bar of soap. "Come here and sit between my knees. You take care of the bath while I wash your hair. Deal?"

"Deal," she said happily as she moved to sit between his naked thighs on the first step. It had to have been her imagination. There was nothing cold or stern about Daniel now. "I don't have much choice if I'm to get out of this tub before I'm smothered by bubbles."

"Lean back. Your hair needs to be wetter." He was leisurely pouring shampoo into her hair, playing with the fragrant foam, making elaborate peaks and twirls. "You would have made a terrific eighteenth-century court lady. Those high white wigs would have suited you."

"I'm glad you think so." She was contentedly running the sponge over her neck and

157

shoulders. "You do have a passion for bubbles, don't you? It's going to take you a long time to rinse all the soap out of my hair. I bet you spent hours in the tub playing with your toys when you were a kid."

"We were allowed precisely seven minutes in the showers at the orphanage. No baths. No rubber ducks," he said matter-of-factly. He was gently rubbing the shampoo into her hair. "It wasn't considered efficient with a mob of hellions like us."

She felt the tears sting her eyes and blinked them away determinedly. "And were you the hellion they thought you?"

"Sure," he said with a shrug. "I was well on my way to reform school when I decided to join the army and see the world." His hands momentarily paused. "The only part of the world I saw on that tour of duty was Nam, and it wasn't a very pretty world." His fingers slowly renewed their massage, but his voice was abstracted. "But I learned to survive in it. I was always a survivor. If I had any special talent, it was the ability to adapt and make situations work for me." His hands fell away from her and his voice was suddenly brisk. "I *did* make them work for me, and there are plenty of people who would criticize some of the ways I did it. I'm not making excuses and I don't intend to. I lived hard because it was the only way I knew how to live."

"You're very defensive," she said softly. "And you shouldn't be. Not with me. I know the kind of man you are. Whatever you did, it was in order to survive." She drew a deep breath. "I understand about surviving."

"Do you?" His voice was oddly choked. "Yes, I think you do." There was a short, poignant silence before he spoke again with deliberate lightness. "Hell, you've certainly managed to survive any number of hazards since I came upon the scene. Hassan, scorpions, even me. I'd say that definitely qualifies you as a survivor." He was standing abruptly. "Now, why don't we see how good you are at surviving" — he lowered his voice to a melodramatic hiss — "the attack of the killer soap bubbles. Go ahead and rinse your hair beneath that faucet while I get you a towel." He strode around the tub and across the room toward the louvered doors of a linen closet beside the shower stall.

He seemed to take a terribly long time choosing a towel, Zilah thought in puzzlement as she rinsed her hair thoroughly and tried to get as much of the foam as she could from her body. He kept his back to her as he went aimlessly through the stack of terry-cloth towels.

"I'm ready to get out."

"I only hope I'm ready to get you out," Daniel murmured beneath his breath as he yanked a white bath sheet from the pile in front of him. His face was set as he strode back toward her, unfolding the towel. She started to rise but had not even reached a standing position before she was enveloped in the terry-cloth sheet and lifted from the tub. There was *nothing* in the least intimate about the thorough rubdown Daniel gave her through the soft material of the towel. When he had finished, he wrapped the towel around her and tucked the ends in at her breasts. Then he grabbed another towel, dried her hair with the same brisk impersonality, and wound the towel around her still damp hair in a makeshift turban. He lifted her in his arms and strode back into the bedroom.

"I know this is terribly inconvenient for you," she said falteringly. "I promise you won't have to do it again. I'm sure I'll be able to manage on my own tomorrow."

"And have me worried out of my skull about you?" He placed her on the bed and covered her with the satin sheet. "You're right. We're going to have to work something

160

else out. I can't go through this every day. I'm not cut out to be a lady's maid."

Those foolish tears were misting her eyes again. It was stupid to feel hurt at his rejection. She tried to smile. "Well, you did an exceptionally good job, even if you did dislike it. It was very kind of you."

"I did a lousy job," he said bluntly. "And there's nothing kind about me. I told you I was a survivor." He ran his hand through his hair. "But I don't think I could survive another session like this. I've got to talk to Philip about getting you a maid until you're fit again."

"There's no reason to disrupt the sheikh's household." She lifted her chin. "And no reason for you to have to take care of me. Your responsibility ended when you brought me to Sedikhan." She met his eyes steadily. "You mustn't think you owe me anything, Daniel. I have no right to demand anything of you."

A variety of emotions were chasing across Daniel's face. Amusement, exasperation, and a fleeting something that might have been tenderness.

"Oh, hell, here we go again." He plopped down on the bed beside her and gathered her hands in his. "We'd better get this in the open right now. I'm no good at beating around the bush." He looked down at her hands clasped in his, a frown creasing his brow. "Look, what happened in the cave was a mistake. We both know that." His thumb was absently rubbing the delicate blue veins of her wrist. "I just want you to know that there's no danger of it ever happening again. I'd like to start out with a clean slate, if it's all right with you. I'm not always a savage."

"You were never savage with me," she said huskily. She was glad he wasn't looking at her. It gave her a moment to absorb the pain his words were knifing into her. She shouldn't have been surprised. She had suspected that the experience in the cave had meant more to her than to Daniel.

His lips twisted. "You're very generous, but I was there, remember? I made a mistake, and I'm just lucky you don't hate my guts." He glanced up at her, a grave expression on his face. "I don't know much about finesse, but I do know about friendship. I'll make you a good friend if you'll let me." His voice was gruff. "I don't have many real friends. It meant a hell of a lot to me when you said you wanted my friendship. I hope the offer still stands."

"It still stands," she said softly. It wasn't what she had hoped for but it was better than nothing. If she worked hard at making that friendship beautiful, it might even be enough. She should know by now that life seldom handed out any prizes. "I'll make you a good friend too, Daniel."

"I know you will." Still holding her gaze with his, he lifted her left palm to his lips and pressed his lips to it gently. "You're a special lady, old friend." He carefully lowered her hand to the bed, as if it were very fragile and might shatter. "Now, what game do you want to play? I brought Trivial Pursuit, Monopoly, and checkers." He was leaning over her, reaching for the pile of boxes he had tossed on her bed.

"It doesn't matter. Anything you like." Her attention had been caught by a long, jagged scar on Daniel's left thigh. It started above his knee and disappeared beneath the frayed edge of his cutoff jeans. "Where did you get that?"

"What?"

Her finger began to trace the puckered scar. He flinched as if she'd burned him. Her eyes flew to his face. "Is it still tender?"

He shook his head. "You just surprised me." His voice was gritty. "It's an old knife wound. I got it years ago."

Her fingers followed the path of the scar up his thigh. "It looks as though it was very deep." His thigh was so hard and muscular.

It was growing even harder under her stroking finger. Was the memory of how he had received that wound causing the tension she felt in him? "Has it healed properly?"

"I think so. It hasn't bothered me since then." The muscles of his thigh were becoming knotted with tension. "Until now."

"Now?" she asked. "Perhaps carrying me all that distance . . ."

"No." He suddenly brushed her hand away and jumped to his feet. "It's fine. Would you like to see the stables and the obstacle course?"

Her eyes widened. "I thought you said we were playing games today."

"I changed my mind," he said through his teeth. "I'm not up to a long, intimate game of Monopoly today. We've got to get out of here." He disappeared into the bathroom and returned with a small portable dryer. He handed it to her. "Blow your hair dry while I hustle the servants to bring the rest of your wardrobe. I particularly specified sports clothes. I hope to heaven they sent jeans and not bikinis. Philip's women usually aren't into sports activity outside of the bedroom."

"But you said I was too weak to tour the stables today."

"You are. I'll carry you."

"But that's ridiculous. I can wa —"

His hand covered her lips. "Zilah, stop arguing." Suddenly he smiled with such warmth that it took her breath away. "Friends have to compromise. I'm giving you what you want, aren't I? Now you have to yield an inch or two as well."

She would have given him anything he wanted to keep him smiling at her with that roguish sweetness. She kissed his palm as gently as he had her own a moment before. "Okay," she said softly. "An inch or so won't hurt me. But only for today, Daniel."

"Only for today." He turned away and headed swiftly toward the door. "We'll take it one day at a time."

6

Daniel lifted Zilah easily to the top rail of the white wooden fence that separated the stableyard from the pasture. "There, you can have a bird's-eye view and still not get in the way of the grooms who are exercising horses. In the morning the stable area has a tendency to get as busy as Churchill Downs before the Kentucky Derby."

Zilah swung her leg over the rail to straddle it. Her gaze traveled eagerly over the long, low stable that was as spotless as the grounds themselves, and then crossed the fence to the lush green of the pasture, which contained a variety of obstacle jumps. "I can see that. What a wonderful place. It reminds me a little of a picture of the Calumet stables I've seen."

"It should," Daniel said dryly. "Philip's father sent a trainer to Calumet to study methods and architecture before having this stable built. Nothing but the best for his only son." He leaned lazily against the fence and lit a cigarette. He blew a thin stream of smoke into the air before studying her with narrowed eyes. "You seem to have livened up a bit. You were very quiet on the way from the house." He looked down at the tip of his cigarette. "Did you get through to your mother?"

The smile faded from her face. "Yes." She looked out at the obstacle course where a groom, who looked little more than a child, was fighting a huge black stallion for control. Despite his size, the boy seemed to be a fine horseman, she thought. "She was very happy. She said she looked forward to seeing me soon." The words were stilted. "She cried."

"That must have been upsetting for you," Daniel said gently. "Are you close?"

"We used to be." She shifted restlessly. "It's been a long time since we've seen each other." She was silent a moment before she spoke again. "She's uncomfortable around me now. I think she still feels a sense of guilt."

"Guilt? Why should she feel guilty?"

"She shouldn't. I tried to tell her that." Zilah's hands clenched unconsciously on the rail. "She blames herself for my . . . illness, for leaving me with my grandmother while she was working. That's one of the reasons I came back to Sedikhan. No one should have to live with guilt like that. I wanted to show her that I'm well and happy now."

"And are you?"

She lifted her chin. "Of course." Her gaze returned again to the boy on the black horse. "Look, he's going to jump him." She frowned. "Aren't the bars awfully high? That must be a six-foot jump."

Daniel's eyes hadn't left her face. "All of Philip's grooms are very competent. You don't have to worry about him."

"He doesn't look old enough to be that competent. He can't be more than eleven or twelve."

His head turned casually to glance out at the pasture. He muttered a low curse, tossed his cigarette to the ground, and crushed it beneath the heel of his boot. He was up on the rail beside her with one swift movement. "Pandora. Philip's going to murder her."

"That's a distinct possibility," Philip El Kabbar said grimly as he joined them on the bar. He had changed to tan riding pants and a white shirt. His worn black boots were of the finest leather, and he looked even more intimidating than he had earlier this morning. "If she doesn't kill herself first."

"Pandora? That's a girl?" Zilah asked, surprised. The slight figure in the black ribbed sweater and frayed jeans appeared to be both wiry and strong. The gray cap pulled down over her eyes completely hid her hair and shadowed her face. It was no wonder Zilah had mistaken her for a boy.

"Her gender is debatable," El Kabbar said. "She doesn't recognize the fact that she's female as yet. She knows only she's either going to win the Olympics or be the greatest jockey since Willie Shoemaker. She hasn't decided which choice will win her ultimate approval."

"Pandora Madchen," Daniel supplied. "She's the daughter of Karl Madchen, the doctor Philip imported to set up a dispensary here at the compound."

"Correction. She's the devil's daughter," the sheikh said. His eyes were narrowed intently on the small figure bent low over the horse's neck as she urged him toward the jump. "The gypsies must have left her."

"Are you going to try to stop her?" Daniel asked curiously. "That's Oedipus, isn't it? I thought you forbade her to ride him."

"I did. But it's too late to stop the jump. If I go out there and try to drag her off now,

169

I'd probably spook him." El Kabbar's eyes were turquoise flints in his set face. "I'll have to wait until she makes the jump and brings him around."

Zilah shivered. El Kabbar's anger was all the more intimidating for its leashed menace. "She's only a child," she offered tentatively.

"She's fifteen, Miss Dabala," El Kabbar said without shifting his eyes from the girl on the horse. "Old enough to obey orders, if not to have a modicum of common sense. One or the other is mandatory here at the stable."

The black stallion's muscles were gathering for the jump, sinews tense and ready. Then he was rising in the air and floating over the jump as if it were three feet instead of six. He landed on the other side with faultless precision.

"Beautiful," Zilah breathed. "She's a magnificent horsewoman, isn't she?"

"The best I've ever known," Philip said. "And the most foolhardy." He jumped down from the fence into the pasture. "I'd suggest you take Miss Dabala back to the house, Daniel. I haven't decided what form Pandora's punishment is going to take, but I just may beat her bottom until she can't sit down." He cast a twisted smile over his shoulder. "I wouldn't want to offend our guest's tender sensibilities."

Zilah watched him stride swiftly toward the girl, who sat waiting across the pasture, her body language practically shouting defiance. "He won't really hurt her, will he?" she asked worriedly. "Perhaps we should phone Dr. Madchen."

Daniel shook his head. "Madchen can't control her. I don't think he even tries. He's let her run wild ever since they arrived in Sedikhan three years ago. Philip is the only one she'll obey." He shrugged. "Sometimes."

He slipped to the ground and reached up to place his big hands on her waist and swing her down. "Come on, I'll take you back to the house. You've seen enough for one day. Tomorrow, if you're stronger, I'll take you for a short ride."

Her troubled gaze returned to the tiny girl on the huge horse. "But I don't think . . ."

He tilted her chin up to meet his eyes. "Philip won't hurt her. He's very decent to her really. He gives her the run of the stables. He lets her trail around after him all over the estate. He's even made sure that she can't come to any harm while running wild in the village." His lips tightened. "But Oedipus is still half wild and too damn strong for her. Philip knows that and he's not about to let her kill herself. In spite of what you think of him, Philip has a hell of a lot of good points. He's honest and scrupulously fair. It may amuse him to act the playboy on occasion, but he also works as hard as any man I've ever met. He's no profligate ruler taking everything from his country and putting nothing back. He's poured millions into that irrigation project, trying to reclaim farmland from the desert. Education and per capita income have soared here since Philip inherited the sheikhdom." He lifted her easily into his arms. "So don't worry about Pandora. Philip isn't going to tie her to a fence post and beat her with a whip. She certainly doesn't need you to mother her. She wouldn't appreciate your interference."

Zilah instantly nestled closer as he carried her swiftly through the stableyard. "She shouldn't be allowed to run wild. It's dangerous for her. Things happen . . ."

She felt his arms tighten around her for the briefest instant. "Nothing is going to happen to Pandora," he said gently. "She's under Philip's protection." He brushed the lightest of kisses on the top of her head. "And nothing will happen to you either. I'll take care of that. Now, just relax and let me get you back to your room. I think you should try to take a nap. I'll wake you for dinner."

"I didn't get to see inside the stables." It was merely a token protest. She was suddenly feeling maddeningly weak, utterly sapped of strength.

"I've never seen a woman so fascinated by four-footed creatures. I never thought I'd be forced on the back of a horse to play guardian angel to a horse-crazy cowgirl."

She glanced up in surprise. "You don't ride?"

He shook his head. "There are some people who don't, you know," he told her solemnly. "I realize it's hard for centaurs like you and Philip to understand, but there are a few of us who even prefer it that way. The last animal I rode was the orneriest mule ever begat on the face of the earth. I was forced to suffer excruciatingly for an entire two-week trip through the Andes." He glared down at her with mock ferocity. "Why the devil are you giggling, you heartless woman? It was a very traumatic experience."

"I'm sure it was." She chuckled. "Don't worry, riding a horse is much more pleasant. I'll teach you. It will be fun, you'll see."

"Will it?" he asked gloomily. "I couldn't

persuade you to recuperate on a nice peaceful cruise around the Mediterranean, I suppose. I have a yacht anchored at the harbor at Marasef, and I assure you that I'm much better at riding the waves than I ever will be a horse."

"Don't be a defeatist," she said with a grin. "You'll be an expert in no time. It's much easier than captaining a ship or blowing up airplanes. Besides, I think I like the idea of being in charge for a change. It's rather nice to know that you're not the master of quite all you survey."

His expression became grave. "Where the hell did you get an idea like that? I don't pretend to be any kind of superbrain. I learn things fairly quickly and my lifestyle has provided me with a variety of skills, but you're probably far better educated than I am." He shrugged. "Hell, I didn't even get my college degree until I retired a couple of years ago. There are probably any number of things you can teach me." He smiled down at her. "And maybe a few I can teach you. It will be interesting to find out anyway, won't it?"

"Yes, I think it will," she said softly. He actually believed that, she realized with a touch of incredulity. He didn't realize how very extraordinary a man he was. He possessed humor, intelligence, and a dogged determination that would always enable him to move mountains. Yet he honestly believed there was nothing unusual about him. "I understand that's a big part of what friendship is all about." She tried to hide the pang of tenderness she was feeling as she nestled nearer to him and closed her eyes. She could hear the throb of his heart more clearly when she shut out the rest of the world. Such a strong vital sound. Just like Daniel himself.

When Zilah opened her eyes she experienced a momentary disorientation that brought her heart leaping to her throat. The slight figure lounging in the wing chair by her bed was totally unfamiliar, and the dusk that pervaded the room threw that stranger into shadow. Dear God, how she hated those shadows. Not this time! Without thinking she scrambled to her knees on the bed, her hands clenched into fists at her sides. "No! Go away."

The slender shadow figure froze in surprise; the trousered leg flung over one arm of the chair halted its lazy swinging. "I can't. Philip won't let me." The hoarse voice was indignant. "It's not that I want to be here, blast it."

"Philip?" Zilah shook her head to clear it, and the shadows of the past disappeared into the mists. Philip El Kabbar. Daniel. "Who are you?"

"Pandora Madchen." The boyish figure straightened in the chair, stretching her booted legs out before her and crossing them at the ankle. Scornful defiance breathed out of every pore. "I'm your new maid," she drawled. "Ma'am."

"My new maid?" Zilah asked blankly. "I've never had an old one. What will I do with you?"

The girl shrugged. "Search me. That's up to you. Scrub your back, brush your hair, junk like that. You're my punishment."

"Punishment?"

"For taking out Oedipus. Philip was mad as hell."

"Yes, he was," Zilah said. "I was there when you took the fence. It was a beautiful jump."

"I've made better," Pandora said. "I saw you on the fence with Philip and Daniel. Which one are you sleeping with?"

"What?"

There was an odd tenseness to the girl's silhouette. "I asked if you were sleeping with Philip. Are you?"

"No. Not that it's any of your business. I

just met Sheikh El Kabbar this morning."

The tenseness left the younger girl's body. "I didn't think so." She was obviously trying to keep the relief from her tone. "He wouldn't have assigned me to you if he'd wanted to keep you happy. He knew I'd probably make your life hell on earth. Is he mad at you or something?"

"Let's just say that he doesn't approve of me." Good heavens, the child was incredible. Amusement was rapidly replacing the resentment that had been Zilah's first reaction. There was a touching childishness beneath Pandora's bravado that reached out to her.

"That's because you're beautiful," Pandora said flatly. "He sleeps with beautiful women but he doesn't like them." She paused before adding with a touch of defiance, "I'm not pretty, but he likes me. He's never said so, but I know he does."

"I'm sure he does," Zilah said gently. "He was very concerned about your safety before you made that jump."

"He was?" The eagerness in the question was naked before Pandora masked it with an offhand shrug. "That's because we're friends. He saved my life, you know."

"No, I didn't know." Zilah brushed a strand of hair from her eyes and settled herself more comfortably against the head-board. She wished there was more light in the room. She'd like to get a better look at this wild child who was intriguing her more every minute.

Pandora nodded. "It was in the first month after I came here with my father. There were some men in the bazaar who were trying to hurt me just because I let loose all the doves in the cages at their stall." She shivered. "They had knives. Philip saved my life. Then he spanked me." Her hand reached up to her throat and she pulled out a gold chain with a round medallion that caught and held the dwindling light in the room. "And then he gave me this."

"A present? That was very kind of him."

"It's not a present," Pandora said indignantly. "It's the sword and the rose. It shows that I belong to him. He said so."

So that was what Daniel meant by Philip extending his protection over the child. "Then he must value you very much."

Pandora lifted her chin. "He does value me. I told you that we were friends. Just because he punishes me now and then doesn't mean he's really angry. He wouldn't bother at all if he didn't like me."

And it was evident Pandora's mischief-making was at least partially a ploy to attract the sheikh's attention in the only way she knew how. It was clear she adored the man far more than he deserved. "Well, I can't say that I like being looked upon as a punishment by your hero," Zilah said dryly. "Nor having you inflicted on me as one either. I don't need a maid and you don't want to be one, so why don't we just call it quits?"

"Are you afraid of me?" There was a note of speculation in Pandora's tone. "You certainly were spooked when you first woke up."

"No," Zilah answered quickly. "Sometimes I have nightmares. I must have been dreaming, and seeing you sitting there startled me."

"I was glad I scared you," Pandora said with the honesty of a child. "I thought it wouldn't hurt to get the upper hand right away since we were going to have to spend some time together."

"But we don't have to spend time together. I'll just tell Sheikh El Kabbar that—"

"It wouldn't do any good," Pandora interrupted with an imperious wave of her right arm. "Philip doesn't change his mind, not ever."

Something dark and liquid had splashed

on the polished white of the mosaic-tile floor when Pandora gestured. Zilah stared at it a moment before she realized what that liquid was.

"You're bleeding!" she said, shocked. "What's wrong with your arm?"

Pandora shrank back farther in the shadows of the wing chair. "Nothing. I scratched it a little."

"Haven't you bandaged it?"

"It isn't serious. I haven't gotten around to it yet."

"If it's bleeding that freely, it should be attended to. Shall I phone your father?"

"No!" Pandora snapped. "It would only make him angry with me again. I told you it wasn't serious."

"If you don't want me to notify your father, then at least let me bandage it." Zilah got out of bed and pulled the girl to her feet. "Come on, I'm not so bad at first aid. I used to help Jess doctor the livestock on the ranch."

"You lived on a ranch?" Surprise made Pandora docile as Zilah led her toward the bathroom. "You don't look like a rancher. You're as beautiful as any of Philip's khadims."

"And good looks aren't allowed in any other profession?" Zilah asked. "I assure you it doesn't get in the way at all. I ride herd on the cattle, brand, mend fences, and I'm a pretty fair horsewoman myself. Not as good as you, but I've won a few blue ribbons in the local horse shows." She chuckled. "And they were far more concerned about my skill at dressage than whether my teeth were prettier than the horse's."

"I'm not terrific at dressage," Pandora said absently. "I'm better at jumping, but I'm working on it. What kind of horse —" They had reached the bathroom door and she broke off. She pulled to a stop. "No, my arm's fine. I don't want to go in there."

"Nonsense," Zilah said. "It will take only a minute." She reached for the doorknob.

Pandora pushed her aside and stepped in front of it. "Then I think I'd better go in first."

"Why on earth?" Zilah asked, puzzled.

There was an indecisive silence before Pandora muttered, "There's a tiger in your bathtub."

"What!"

"It's only a little tiger," Pandora said hurriedly. "Just a cub really. I was keeping it in the stable, but I couldn't leave him there with no one to take care of him. Horses get nervous around cats, and someone would have been sure to discover him."

"So you put him in my bathtub." Zilah's voice was dazed. "Did you think I wouldn't find him? I assure you I use the bathroom with moderate frequency."

"It was all I could think of," Pandora said. "I couldn't let those poachers get hold of him again."

"What poachers? Why do I feel I've entered the twilight zone?"

"Oh, do you watch 'Twilight Zone'? Philip has all the episodes on video cassettes. They're very interesting, aren't —"

"Pandora," Zilah interrupted, pronouncing each syllable very distinctly. "I'm not interested in Philip's passion for 'Twilight Zone.' What poachers?"

"There were some poachers in the bazaar last week. Philip wouldn't have stood for it, but they move around from place to place and sometimes he doesn't know. They had the skins of a few adult tigers and they had penned up Androcles in a cage. I guess they were waiting until he was older before they butchered him. So I waited until dark that night and then sneaked in and stole him."

"You stole a tiger?" Zilah asked faintly. "That must have been interesting."

"I get along with animals," Pandora said simply. "They trust me."

"Is that scratch on your arm from your

friend Androcles? If so, I wouldn't say that demonstrated a high degree of friendliness."

"You couldn't expect him not to be frightened. I had to smuggle him into the house under a coat. Naturally, he clawed me a little."

"Naturally," Zilah echoed, shaking her head in wonder.

"Are you going to tell Philip?" Pandora asked tensely. She raised her chin. "Not that he'd care. He likes me better than he does you."

"That wouldn't be difficult," Zilah said dryly. "And I haven't decided yet what I'm going to do. Suppose we take a look at your friend Androcles and see just how much of a danger he is." She wouldn't be surprised to see a full-grown tiger in the bathroom. Or, for that matter, to see nothing at all. It could be an elaborate joke. She was beginning to believe anything could be possible with Pandora Madchen.

It wasn't a joke.

The tiger cub was curled up fast asleep on a bath towel in the center of the pink and ivory sunken tub. When Zilah flipped on the light, he opened one sleepy eye and then rolled over on his side.

"Isn't he cute?" Pandora asked. "Just like a big pussy cat."

"Adorable." At least he wasn't full-grown as Zilah had half feared. He *was* rather sweet. "However, he doesn't seem to have a very developed sense of self-preservation. I think he's gone back to sleep already."

"Animals sense things. He knows we wouldn't hurt him. Can we keep him?"

"Pandora, this isn't like those doves you let out of their cages," Zilah said. "This charming little pussy cat is going to grow up to be a dangerous animal. How could you —" Her glance moved from the tiger cub to the face of the girl beside her. "Good heavens, you're *gorgeous!* I thought you said you weren't pretty."

"I'm *not* pretty." Pandora said fiercely. "I'm straight as a stick and I have horrible hair. And," she added triumphantly, "I have freckles."

She did have freckles. A golden dusting across the bridge of a small, perfect nose in a face with the most beautifully classic bone structure Zilah had ever seen. Huge midnight-dark eyes were surrounded by lashes of equal darkness. The "horrible hair" was chopped rather than cut into a boyish style that looked like it had been caught in an eggbeater. Still, the color and texture were magnificent. It was a shade of blond that was close to silver and it caught and reflected all the light in the room. She did lack curves, but she was as fine-boned and athletically graceful as the tiger cub in the bathtub. Good heavens, if she was this beautiful at fifteen, she would be unbelievable at twenty. Yet her denial of that beauty held a puzzling element of desperation. Then the light dawned. Philip El Kabbar didn't like or trust beautiful women, according to Pandora. Therefore Pandora refused to be beautiful.

"My mistake," Zilah said solemnly. "I didn't notice the freckles."

"Well, the light is pretty bad in here," Pandora conceded. She pointed to the tiger cub. "I know I can't keep him indefinitely. He'll have to be sent to a wildlife reserve, but I thought it wouldn't hurt to keep him for a little while." Her expression took on a poignant wistfulness. "I've never had a pet before. We always moved around too much before we came here. I thought just for a little while . . ."

Zilah felt a melting helplessness that boded no good for her common sense. "Well, perhaps for a day or so it wouldn't do any harm," she said reluctantly. "I probably wouldn't be using the tub anyway. I usually prefer to take a shower." She suddenly ran her hand distractedly through her hair. "Oh, Lord, what am I saying? I think I've just accepted a tiger as a roommate."

"I think so too." Pandora's grin lit her face with breathless beauty. "You can't back out now. It will be fine. I'll make sure he doesn't get in your way and I'll do all the cleaning myself. I'll keep all the servants out of your room and get a couple of blankets and bunk in here with him during the night. Philip assigned me a guest room next door but it doesn't have a tub like this or I would have kept Androcles in there. He won't be any trouble at all."

"I'll believe it when I see it." Zilah made a face. "Now, let me look at your arm and see what your harmless little pussy cat has done to you."

Pandora silently held her right arm out. There was a hand towel tied around her forearm in a make-shift bandage. When Zilah removed it she inhaled sharply. There were several deep claw marks on the girl's thin arm, three of which were still bleeding. Zilah shook her head. "Just a little scratch," she murmured caustically as she slid back the mirror above the vanity to reveal a medicine chest. "You should have disinfected those claw marks right away. For a doctor's daughter you're very ignorant of primary first aid."

"My father and I don't get along very well. He never got around to teaching me much about anything," Pandora said with a shrug. "He's never liked me."

"Sometimes it's difficult to tell if someone likes you or not," Zilah said gently as she took a roll of gauze and a bottle of antiseptic from the shelf and closed the sliding mirrored doors. "People aren't always easy to read."

"I can tell," Pandora said fiercely. Her eyes lowered to watch Zilah carefully wash the scratches. "It doesn't matter. I don't care anyway."

Zilah opened the antiseptic. "This will sting."

Pandora inhaled sharply but made no other indication of pain as Zilah applied the antiseptic to the raw wound. Her dark eyes were narrowed intently on Zilah's face. "*You* like me. I can tell that too."

"Yes, I like you." Zilah looked up from winding the gauze about Pandora's thin, wiry arm. "Which only goes to prove I have temporary attacks of insanity. I have an idea you're going to bring me nothing but trouble."

"I like you too," Pandora said awkwardly. "At first, I thought you were pretty flighty. But you're not afraid of tiger cubs, or blood,

187

or even Philip. The only thing you're afraid of are those nightmares."

"I imagine you could dredge up a few more things that I'm nervous about." Zilah stepped back after taping the gauze bandage firmly in place. "If those wounds start to fester, we'll have to go to your father for antibiotics."

"We'll see," Pandora said noncommittally. "It will probably heal all right. I'm pretty tough."

With a streak of vulnerability a mile wide, Zilah thought. "I'll change the dressing every day until we see how it's doing," she said firmly as she opened the mirrored panel and replaced the first aid materials on the shelf. "I'm pretty tough too." Then, as if to belie the statement, she suddenly swayed and had to grab the counter of the vanity to keep from falling. "Oh, damn!"

Pandora's arm was swiftly around her waist, steadying her. "What's wrong?" Her brow was creased in a troubled frown. "Are you okay?"

"I'm fine," Zilah said, taking a deep breath. "I guess I've been on my feet too long. I forgot all about being a convalescent for a little while." She made a face. "Unfortunately, nature has a way of reminding you. I was stung by a scorpion yesterday morning and I can't seem to get my strength back."

"I didn't know you'd been ill." Pandora's face was stricken. "Come on, I'll help you get back to bed." Pandora's grip was surprisingly strong for so slight a girl and she was almost lifting instead of supporting Zilah as she whisked her across the room. "You should have told me. Don't worry, I'll take care of you. Is that why Philip wanted me to act as your maid?"

"I imagine you were right the first time. I doubt if he was really concerned about me."

"Probably not." Pandora pushed her gently down on the bed and leaned forward to switch on the bedside lamp. "You just rest here and I'll go get you something to eat."

"You don't need to bother. Daniel said he would bring me something after my nap. He should be here anytime now."

"Then I'll go find him and tell him not to bother. You can see him in the morning. You're too weak to have to deal with visitors tonight."

"I am?" Zilah asked blankly.

Pandora nodded with authority. "You need a good meal and an early night." She scowled. "I'll even brush your hair and help you put on your creams and junk. You wouldn't want him to see you with all that slippery stuff all over you."

"I use only a little moisturizer," Zilah said absently. "And he's seen me look a lot worse."

Pandora's eyes were speculative. "Is he the one you're sleeping with? You don't have to worry about my getting in the way. After you're well again you won't even know I'm around, but you shouldn't have to worry about that sex stuff when you're sick."

"Thank you," Zilah said meekly. "But Daniel and I are only friends. You won't have to use such discretion. He's probably the one who told Philip I needed a maid."

"You're not sleeping with either one of them?" Pandora shook her head. "How peculiar."

Evidently in Pandora's experience, good-looking women didn't sleep alone. It wasn't surprising with a man like Philip El Kabbar as a mentor. "Not really." Zilah smothered a smile. "I understand it can be quite restful. I thought I'd try it. Merely as an experiment, you understand."

"You're laughing at me," Pandora accused Zilah with an uncertain frown. "I don't know if I like that." Then she grinned mischievously. "Oh, what the hell, it's no worse than what I was going to do to you."

"Something worse than a tiger in my bathtub?" Zilah asked warily.

Pandora had turned and was striding swiftly toward the door. "Only if I found it was Philip you were sleeping with," she said soothingly over her shoulder. "Otherwise I was going to forget all about it."

"Forget about what?"

Pandora paused as she opened the door, and there was a touch of fierceness beneath the mischief in her eyes. "I was going to wait until you were in the middle of . . ." She paused delicately, and then came out with an obscene Anglo-Saxon term that caused Zilah's eyes to widen in shock. "And then I was going to sneak in and drop Androcles on top of both of you." She smiled with infinite satisfaction. "I'd say that would do the job of spoiling the mood."

"I think you could count on it," Zilah said faintly as she watched the door swing shut behind the girl. Throughout this entire weird encounter she had been feeling sympathy for Pandora in her passionate attachment for the sheikh. Now she began to wonder if she shouldn't feel a bit sorry for Philip El Kabbar.

7

The meadow of wild poppies seemed to stretch into forever and beyond. The silken scarlet of the petals was still trembling beneath the weight of the crystal dew and the breeze of dawn whipped across them like the murmur of a lover.

"It's beautiful." Zilah's voice was as hushed as the world around them. The sun was just rising above the tamarisk trees in the distance, streaking the sky with hazy pink and gold. "I've never seen such heavenly colors." She lifted her face and let the cool breeze touch her cheeks, inundating her with the sheer sensual pleasure of sight, touch, and scent. She breathed in the fragrance of the rich earth blended subtly with the tamarisk and the poppy. It was so intoxicating, it almost made her dizzy. "Why didn't you bring me here before?"

"I didn't want to venture outside the pasture," Daniel said as he swung out of the saddle and flung the reins over the head of the big bay he had been riding. "I wasn't sure you were strong enough. Even though this meadow is only a little beyond the tamarisks on the far side of the pasture, I'm not a good enough rider to get you out of trouble if you tired. Old Dobbin, here, and I still aren't sure we trust each other."

She shook her head. "You've done marvelously well for having ridden only a week." She slipped off her gray mare into his arms, automatically steeling herself for the little sensual shock that always came when he touched her. Friends. Most of the time it was easier to remember the ground rules he had laid down. Today it wasn't quite so easy in this paradise of sunrise and poppies.

He shook his head. "We both know I'll never be anything but an adequate rider. The only reason I have as much control as I do over this trusty steed is that I have a pair of powerful legs I can wrap around him to show who's boss."

She smiled with an effort. "Actually, I think Pandora intimidated you into being overcareful. I've found she has the devotion of a she-wolf when her maternal instincts are aroused. She's been practically smothering me with attention this past week."

"I know, she won't even let me in your

room," Daniel said sourly. "It's practically thrown Philip into shock. He suspects you of using hypnosis on her."

"Just kindness," Zilah said quietly. "He should try it sometime."

"I think he's a little afraid to encourage her. Pandora can be overwhelming." He met her eyes steadily. "Perhaps not encouraging her is his own way of being kind to her. He doesn't want to hurt her."

Was there a double meaning in that explanation? Had she been so transparent that he thought she needed a warning? She wasn't very accomplished at hiding her feelings. "The hurt will come anyway." She turned away. "And at least she'd have something to remember. A good memory to temper the bad ones." She glanced over her shoulder to smile at him. "And I want to create a beautiful memory right now. Have you ever run through a field of wild poppies, Daniel?"

He shook his head. A wavering ray of light tangled in his hair, turning it into silken flame. He was dressed in a blue chambray shirt that stretched over his broad shoulders and clung to his trim waist. His worn jeans were tucked into suede boots. It was another memory to hold on to: Daniel with the sunrise in his hair. "I can't say that I have."

"Neither have I. Come on. Let's do it!" She turned and raced into the meadow. The wind was cool and stinging on her cheeks and the colors and scents flowed around her in a blur that shimmered with exquisite radiance. She could hear Daniel's footsteps behind her, the harsh sound of his breathing. Her own lungs were hurting but she didn't want to stop. She never wanted to stop.

"Zilah, that's enough."

She could hear a note of grimness in Daniel's voice that shocked her, and her pace faltered slightly.

"If you don't stop, so help me I'm going to tackle you."

She halted and turned to face him. "What's wrong?"

He overtook her in two strides. His hands fell heavily on her shoulders. "What's wrong is that you're acting like a crazy woman. You've been ill, remember? Now you're behaving as if you're training for the Olympic one-hundred-yard dash." He shook her slightly. "I thought you were trying to make it clear to the other side of the meadow."

"Well, why didn't you stop me before? I got a little carried away, but I'm not unreasonable."

"Because I couldn't catch you, dammit."

His lips curved ruefully. "I'm built more for endurance than for speed."

She flung back her head and laughed joyously. "Daniel, there's no one like you. You always speak the exact truth no matter how it may hurt your ego." There was a strange look on his face that caused the laughter to fade from hers. "What's wrong now?"

"I've never heard you laugh before," he said simply. "I like it."

She felt more breathless than when she had been running. "Then I'll try to do it more often. I didn't realize that I was being such a sad sack." She fell to her knees in the poppies. "Maybe you're right, my legs do feel a little weak."

He knelt down beside her and leaned back on his heels. "Mine too." His eyes were narrowed on her face. "You're never gloomy. You're always smiling and serene." He reached out and touched her cheek with a gentle finger. "And beautiful. Always beautiful, old friend."

Another memory. *Old friend.* This time it sounded like a lover's endearment again.

"Pandora wouldn't consider that a compliment," she said shakily. "She thinks beautiful women are good only for one purpose." Her lashes veiled her eyes as she reached out to pluck one of the poppies that surrounded them. She wished she hadn't said that. It brought too vivid an image to mind. Daniel, strong and naked, making love to her in the big bed in her room with its cool satin sheets. She had never really seen him loving her. There had been only the darkness and the passion. Yet it had been more than enough at the time. She hurriedly tried to blank out the thought. She mustn't ask too much. These past ten days had been beautiful too, and they had to be enough. Daniel had been as kind and gentle as an older brother to a beloved little sister. A very fragile little sister, however, she thought wistfully. It was almost as if he were afraid to touch her even in the most platonic way. Couldn't he see that she was almost entirely well now? He might no longer desire her, but even casual friends exchanged a casual caress now and then.

They had grown close in so many ways. They had talked, played games, shared meals and experiences. She felt she knew him better than anyone in her entire life. He was part of her life now. How was she going to stand it when he considered her well enough to return to Zalandan and went about his own life? Would he visit her occasionally? Probably. He considered her a good friend, and Daniel was very loyal to his friends.

"You're not smiling anymore. What are you thinking about?"

"Zalandan." One finger smoothed the silky petals of the poppy on her lap. "I called my mother last night. David and Billie are home from New York. She said he was very upset that no one had told him about the hijacking. He wanted to know when I was coming home."

"Then he can keep on wondering," Daniel said harshly. "You're not well enough to travel yet. Dr. Madchen told you that yesterday, didn't he?"

"Yes, he told me that." The decision had brought a surge of pure joy. "But it's only a matter of time until he releases me. I feel so well now. David was surprised he hadn't done it already. He said he was going to call him and discuss the case with him."

"We've done fine without your precious David's interference so far. You can tell him to mind his own damn business." Then, when he saw the shock on her face, his lips twisted. "But you couldn't tell him that, could you? You owe him too much. He's your best friend."

She shook her head. "He's my good friend," she corrected him softly. "Not my best one. Not anymore. You're my best friend, Daniel."

He went still. Something flared in his face and was quickly masked. "How is Bradford going to take that? You've been his special property for a long time."

"David doesn't believe that caring should be some kind of competition. He's a very beautiful human being, Daniel. There are times when he reminds me of a high mountain lake, clean and deep and crystal-clear. I want you to know him."

"I'm not sure I want to," he said tersely. "Unlike Bradford, I'm intensely competitive, and I might find meeting such a paragon a little hard on my ego. You could never compare me to a blasted mountain lake."

"It shouldn't bother you." She smiled gently. "You're something of a paragon yourself. It's true you're no clear mountain lake. You're more like the sea. Rough and powerful and yet capable of sustaining life, even giving life. I think you'd get along very well with David."

His expression was stunned. "I'll try," he said gruffly. "I know he means a lot to you. That's part of my problem. I've always been a jealous bastard." He grimaced. "I suppose it goes back to when I was a kid and had to grab what I wanted and hold on tight to keep it from being taken away from me. I guess I'm still grabbing."

"There's no need to grab what I'm willing to give," Zilah said. She reached out a hand to touch his arm. He tensed and she could feel the muscles bunch beneath her fingertips. She felt an aching pain at that unconscious physical rejection but she tried to keep it from her voice. "I don't believe in half measures, Daniel. If you care for someone, you give everything they want or need."

His harsh laugh held a note of pain. "That's right. You told me you'd sleep with Bradford in a minute if he asked it of you. That it wasn't important. I take it I'm now being sheltered under that same umbrella of generosity with the same carte blanche?"

She froze, her eyes widening. "If that's what you want," she managed to get out.

"Well, it's *not* what I want." His hands were unconsciously clenched into fists. His blue eyes were blazing in his pale face. "And it is important, dammit. Your body has value just as your mind and spirit do. You shouldn't treat it as something to throw away on anyone who reaches out to take it."

She felt as if he'd struck her. "It's not like that," she said shakily. "I'm not like that. Not with just anyone, Daniel."

"Oh, God, I know that." The words were

wrenched out of him. His hands reached out to cup her shoulders. They were trembling. "It just drives me crazy when you say something like that. You're so damn beautiful. Inside and out you're *beautiful.* Don't you know that? The world out there can be so dark and ugly, and you shine like a candle in that darkness. People like me need to know that there are little flickers of hope out there. So, dammit, shine *proudly,* Zilah."

She was staring at him with her mouth slightly open. She felt as if she'd received the Nobel Peace Prize. She closed her lips and smiled at him with a radiant warmth that lit her face. "Candles and lakes and seas. We both seem to be full of metaphors this morning." She glanced behind her at the field of poppies bending in the breeze. "It must be the surroundings. Poppies have to be one of the most beautiful flowers on earth." She shook her head in wonder. "And I used to hate them."

"Zilah . . ."

"It's strange, isn't it? But the fruit of the poppy is opium, you know."

"I know." Daniel's hands tightened on her shoulders. His expression was guarded and intent.

"Heroin. I couldn't stand the thought of that ugliness coming from such beauty. It took me a long time to come to terms with the idea. But I gradually began to be more objective about it." She looked down at the poppy clutched in her hand. "There is never just one side to anything. Opium can bring evil and yet it can stop agony as well. A poppy can beget horror, yet it can lift the heart with its beauty. Now I just try to embrace the beauty and live with the knowledge of the darker side." She moistened her lips nervously and looked up to meet his eyes. "I know I seem to be rambling on, but I'm trying to tell you something. I probably should have told you before, but it still hurts me to talk about it."

"Then don't tell me," he said roughly. "I don't need to know. I don't have any right to know if it's going to hurt you."

"But David knows," she said, her expression troubled. "I don't want you to feel I'm keeping something from you that I'd share with him."

"I'm not that competitive. I don't need you to bare your soul to me to give me an advantage over Bradford."

Relief surged through her, making her almost light-headed. "All right. Not now, then. I'll tell you soon though."

His hand reached out to brush his knuckles over her lips to the curve of her jaw in a gentle caress. "When you're ready, I'll still be here to listen." His hand dropped away and he was suddenly on his feet. "But, if I'm going to make sure you're still around, I'd better get you back to the house and see that you get some breakfast." His hand reached down and he pulled her up. "You're still on the sick list."

She shook her head. Daniel was being very much the big brother again. Yet she wasn't as discouraged as she might have been. The morning had been so full of beauty and revelation that it had planted a tiny seed of hope. Daniel *did* care about her. Perhaps even more than he realized. If she nurtured that seed, perhaps it would blossom as beautifully as this lovely poppy in her hand.

She reached up and tucked the green stem of the flower into the top buttonhole of Daniel's blue shirt. "Yes, let's get back," she said lightly. "Or Pandora just may swipe Oedipus again and come looking for us!"

Pandora appeared surprisingly unconcerned when Zilah walked into the room. She was sitting cross-legged on the Oriental carpet by the bed scratching Androcles's belly and she glanced up with a grin. "Will you look at that? I think he's going to start to purr any minute."

"Could be." Zilah dropped down beside her on the floor and gingerly patted the cub's head. "I think he's grown in the last week."

Pandora nodded. "I know he has," she said sadly. "It won't be long before I have to give him up." She brightened. "But not yet." She picked the cub up and put him over her shoulder like a baby about to be burped, her hand lazily scratching the tiger's furry nape. "Have you had breakfast?"

"Daniel and I ate in the breakfast room when we came back from our ride." Zilah raised a brow quizzically. "You seem to be very casual all of a sudden. What happened to all that mother-hen clucking?"

"You're well now." Pandora shrugged. "You don't need it anymore. I could tell when my father examined you yesterday that it was only a matter of form. He didn't think you were ill any longer."

"Well, then why wouldn't he release me?" Zilah asked, puzzled. "You have to be mistaken."

"I'm not mistaken." Pandora's lips curved in a bittersweet smile. "I've learned to read my father very well over the years. I don't know why he didn't release you, but it wasn't because you weren't entirely well. Maybe Philip told him not to. My father

204

likes the lifestyle Philip provides here in Sedikhan. He does what Philip tells him to do."

"I hardly think your friend, the sheikh, is craving my company to that extent," Zilah said dryly. "Though I admit he's been very courteous when our paths happened to cross lately. I'm hardly on his list of favorite people."

"But Daniel Seifert is on that list," Pandora said calmly. "And Daniel wants you."

Zilah felt a shock jolt through her. "Daniel is my friend," she said huskily.

"He wants to go to bed with you," Pandora said bluntly. "He watches you all the time. I bet he can scarcely keep his hands off you." She lowered her lashes so their length veiled her eyes. "I know how a man looks at a woman when he wants to sleep with her. I've seen it often enough."

Philip and his many khadims? Zilah felt a surge of aching sympathy for the child-woman who was Pandora.

"You're wrong about Daniel," she said gently. "He doesn't want me in that way."

Pandora shrugged. "You'll find out. I don't know what you're so uptight about. You want him too." She glanced up suddenly. Her magnificent raven-dark eyes were sharp as diamonds. "Don't you?"

Zilah didn't answer for a moment. "Yes, I want him," she finally said softly. "But I also love him. The two don't come in separate packages for me, Pandora." It was strange to say the words aloud. She felt lighter, as if a burden had been lifted from her.

"Nor for me either," Pandora whispered, rubbing her cheek against the cub's soft fur. She closed her eyes. "Isn't that funny? Philip never has a problem like that. Neither does my mother."

"Your mother?" Zilah had somehow thought Pandora's mother was dead. The girl had never spoken of her before.

"My mother's on her sixth husband now," Pandora said. "She's one of the beautiful ones." She opened her eyes. "She's an actress. Not a very good one, but then, she doesn't have to be."

"Your parents are divorced?"

"Since I was three. My father hates her," Pandora said dispassionately. "I don't hate her. She isn't cruel or heartless or anything like that. She's just selfish and likes to have a good time. She insisted I come and visit her in Hollywood four years ago and she was quite nice to me."

Quite nice to her own daughter? Somehow the phrase was more poignant than a brutal condemnation would have been. "You were probably very easy to be nice to."

Pandora shook her head and suddenly the sadness was gone from her face. She grinned mischievously. "No, I was hell on wheels even then. She was glad to see me leave. Did you know that according to myth, Vulcan created Pandora out of clay?"

"No, I didn't know that."

"Well, he did. But Philip says I definitely don't have feet of clay. He says they have to be hooves." Her eyes were twinkling. "I asked him if he meant a horse's hooves or Satan's cloven hooves, but he wouldn't tell me. He said that either concept would fit admirably."

"It sounds like him." Zilah got to her feet. "I have to leave now. I promised to meet Daniel at the pool at eleven for a swim. Do you have enough books to keep you occupied or should I go to the library and pick up a few more?"

"I have enough." Pandora's expression was suddenly speculative. "I may give Androcles a bath. Tigers are supposed to be able to swim, aren't they? I wonder if it's instinctive or if they have to be taught."

"Oh, dear, now you're giving him swimming lessons?"

"If he's going into a wildlife reserve, he has to have all the skills to survive," Pandora said earnestly. "I'm sure it won't take long. Androcles is very clever."

"You don't mind if I use the bathroom first to change into my swimming suit and braid my hair?" Zilah asked politely. "If it wouldn't be too much bother?"

"Am I being pushy?" Pandora asked a little uncertainly. "You don't really mind our being here, do you?"

Zilah tousled the top of Pandora's silky head affectionately. "I like having you here," she said as she turned toward the bathroom. "You're good company." She sighed. "I'm even growing fond of that blasted tiger cub."

Zilah had reached the bathroom door when Pandora spoke behind her. "Daniel *does* want you. Maybe if he doesn't love you now, it might come afterward." Her voice was wistful. "You might have a chance, at least."

"That's assuming that you're right." Zilah kept her voice firmly under control. "And you're not right, Pandora. Not this time." The door closed softly behind her.

Daniel replaced the receiver of the telephone and turned away from the desk to accept the drink Philip was holding out to him. "Three down, one to go."

"Donahue?"

Daniel nodded. "They captured three of the terrorists this afternoon trying to cross the border back into Said Ababa." He took a sip of brandy. "Hassan wasn't with them. They'd had a slight difference of opinion and split up." Daniel smiled grimly. "These three decided they wanted to stay alive."

"You think he's still on your trail?"

"Probably," Daniel said. "According to his dossier, Hassan is almost as fanatical as his brother. He won't give up easily. Starting tomorrow I want a guard on Zilah's door." He made a face. "Not that she'll need it with Pandora staying in her room. I haven't even been permitted through that sacred portal since she arrived on the scene."

"Really?" Philip's arm halted midway in the act of lifting his own drink to his lips. "That's curious. I knew she was displaying a most unusual devotion, but I can't see Pandora as a chaperone. I would have thought you would have objected more vigorously. I take it you're not sleeping with the lady?"

Daniel was silent.

"Even more curious," Philip said. "It's not like you to waste opportunities. You wouldn't want to tell me why you've developed this superhuman restraint at this stage in your life?"

"No, I don't think I would," Daniel said quietly. "I don't think it's something that you would understand."

Philip drained his glass. "You're probably right." He set the glass down on the desk. "But I do understand the little dragon I put in charge of your chaste princess, and it's not in character for her to be overly protective of anyone."

"Except you," Daniel suggested softly.

Philip inclined his head mockingly. "Except me," he conceded. He turned to go. "You'll get your guard, but I think I'll just go see why Pandora is suddenly behaving with such zealous propriety." He paused at the door. "Would you care to come with me?"

Daniel shook his head. "Clancy is interrogating the prisoners now. He's going to phone me back if they're able to pry Hassan's hiding place out of them. Tell Zilah I'll come and let her know the details as soon as I get the call. She'd better have dinner without me."

"I'm sure if anyone can extract the information, he can." Philip drawled. "A very thorough man, your Clancy Donahue."

"He'd better be damn thorough," Daniel said wearily as he sat down in the oversized chair facing the desk. "I want this over and done with."

"You're on edge," Philip said. "I under-stand celibacy has a way of doing that to a man." He smiled faintly. "Personally, I haven't been so foolish as to indulge in that idiocy since I was fourteen, so I wouldn't know."

"Philip." Daniel leaned his head back against the high back of the chair and tried to relax the tense muscles of his shoulders. "Go to hell."

Philip laughed. "That's the second time in the last ten days I've been designated to the fire and brimstone. Do you suppose I'm not as charming as I've been led to believe?" He held up his hand. "Don't answer that. It's much more comfortable to be left with my illusions."

Daniel's hand tightened on the arm of his chair as the door closed behind the other man. Then he consciously forced himself to relax. He shouldn't have been so short with Philip. If Philip hadn't possessed a puckish sense of humor beneath that mocking ar-rogance, he might have taken offense. And despite his feelings regarding Zilah's pres-ence here, Philip had acted the true friend. He had offered hospitality as well as the protective cloak of power that surrounded every guest of Sheikh El Kabbar.

Daniel suddenly grinned as he remembered Philip's last remark. It was probably Zilah who had been the first to consign Philip to the fiery depths. He wouldn't put it past her. There was strength and spirit in her that ran like a powerful underground river beneath that beautiful serene surface. He only wished he could concentrate on those lovely spiritual qualities without being distracted by the tempting surface. Like Philip, he wasn't accustomed to celibacy, and his willpower had been stretched to the limit in the last ten days. He felt like someone had kicked him in the stomach every time she brushed casually against him. He was sure he hadn't slept more than a few hours a night during the entire time. His nerves were so frayed and raw that it was a wonder he had been able to exercise any control at all.

However, he had succeeded in maintaining that avuncular façade, judging from Zilah's touching declaration this morning. He was her best friend. He had to hold on to that. He had gained her trust; he mustn't blow everything because he was so hot for her he was ready to explode. It might take months, even years, before she was ready to give herself because it was what *she* wanted, not because of that unselfish generosity that seemed ingrained in her. He could wait. At least, he hoped he could. This afternoon when she had appeared at the pool in that French-cut swim suit, he hadn't been sure. He'd been so aroused he'd had to spend the entire session in the pool to keep from scaring the hell out of her.

He finished his drink and leaned forward to set his glass on the desk. Of course he could wait. All he had to do was avoid swimming pools, and bathtubs, and the sight of Zilah on a horse or walking across the room. It would be a real piece of cake.

He settled back in the chair and stretched his legs out before him. It was just as well that he had to wait here for Clancy's call. He was in no shape to play the platonic friend tonight. He had to gather his reserves and repair his defenses before he faced Zilah again for any extended period. Hell, at this rate he might even have to take up yoga and contemplate his navel or something, he thought. Maybe it would take his mind off other portions of his anatomy.

8

Zilah's eyes widened in surprise as she opened the door.

"May I come in?" Philip El Kabbar asked politely. "You'll notice my manners have improved. I even knocked. I think that deserves a reward."

"Yes, of course." Zilah tightened the belt of her white satin robe and stepped back. "I wasn't expecting you."

"According to Daniel, your security has been so tight that you shouldn't have been expecting anyone." Philip's turquoise-colored eyes were fixed on her face. "Where is the little tigress?"

"Tigress?" Zilah asked faintly. Oh, dear heavens, he knew! She should have known Pandora would never be able to pull it off.

The shiekh frowned. "Pandora," he said impatiently. "I understand she's been guarding you like a tiger with her only cub. Where is she?"

"Oh, Pandora." Zilah felt weak with relief. "She's in the bathroom. I think she's rinsing out a few things. I'll go and get her."

"Rinsing out a few things?" Philip's lips twisted skeptically. "Pandora? That's a rather tame occupation for her. Have you worked some magic to turn her into a docile lady's maid? I think I'll be very displeased if you have. That's not why I sent her to you."

"I know," Zilah said quietly. "I'm sorry to disappoint you, but we get along very well. She's a charming child and I like her very much."

"Then it's obviously time I sent her away," Philip said as he closed the door and leaned against it. He was dressed in dark trousers and shirt that outlined his lean, tough body and was as maddeningly attractive as he was outrageous. "Her stay here was supposed to be a punishment. Clearly it hasn't turned out that way."

"What do you have in mind?" Zilah asked stormily. "Perhaps you could throw her into the dungeon instead."

"Yes, I could. There is one, you know. Thank you for the suggestion," Philip drawled. "I'll consider it."

"You're utterly impossible. Do you realize that? You're a complete anachronism."

He smiled. "But I have the power to get

away with it. In the end, that's the bottom line. Haven't you found that to be true?" His smile vanished. "And I don't appreciate your taking it upon yourself to defend her from my very righteous wrath. Pandora is my property. She'll tell you that herself."

"Only because she mistakenly thinks the sun rises and sets with you. She's lived for the past several years in an environment entirely under your control. What do you think her reaction will be when she goes out into the world and finds out all men aren't self-indulgent barbarians?"

Something flickered in his face. Anger? Pain? It was difficult to tell, for it was gone so quickly. "It's hard to anticipate Pandora's reactions. She seldom thinks and acts like other women." He paused. "Yet. She's still in the embryo stage." He straightened. "Now, if you've quite finished trying to puncture my arrogance, I'll go fetch your poor victimized little friend." He started across the room.

Zilah instinctively ran to stand before the bathroom door. "No. I'll get her. You stay right here."

Philip stopped, his gaze taking in the trace of panic in her face. He shook his head. "I don't think so," he said slowly. He grasped her shoulders and lifted her aside. "I find

I'm suddenly very eager to view this newly docile Pandora at her housekeeping duties." He turned the knob. "Very eager indeed."

Zilah said hurriedly, "I don't think —" She broke off.

It was too late. He had thrown open the door and she could tell by the stunned expression on his face that the jig was very definitely up.

She shifted to peer over his shoulder and almost groaned aloud. Ribbons! Where on earth had Pandora gotten the pink ribbons?

Somewhere, evidently, for she was sitting in the center of the sunken tub dressed in her usual jeans and ribbed cotton sweater. It was Androcles who was haute couture with an enormous pink satin bow tied around his striped tail. Pandora was in the process of tying another around his neck when she casually glanced up. She froze into statuelike stillness.

"A tigress! My God, a tigress! No wonder you did a double-take when I said that," Philip exclaimed.

Pandora was rallying quickly. "He's a male, actually. His name is Androcles. Hello, Philip."

"A tiger," he repeated, dazed. "You've had a tiger in the bathtub for the last week?"

Pandora lifted her chin defiantly. "Well,

it's your own fault, Philip. It was your idea for me to come here. I couldn't just abandon him, could I?"

"Abandon a tiger?" Philip asked blankly. "How does one abandon a tiger?"

Pandora got to her feet and gathered Androcles protectively in her arms. "He's only a baby. He didn't even know how to swim until I taught him."

"You taught him to *swim?*" He shook his head as if to clear it.

Pandora frowned. "Really, Philip, I wish you'd listen. I think I'm making everything perfectly clear."

"Oh, perfectly." His lips were twitching uncontrollably. "I don't know why I appear to be so thick-headed tonight. I suppose I'm more accustomed to thinking of a tiger in the jungle than in the bathtub. You'll have to forgive my lack of adaptability." He suddenly threw back his head and laughed uproariously. It was some time before his laughter dwindled to a chuckle. His blue-green eyes were still twinkling as he slowly shook his head. "I've heard of a tiger in the tank, of course. But, as usual, you've gone a step further, Pandora. Why should I have expected anything else?"

Pandora breathed a sigh of relief. "You're not angry with me?"

"I'm furious," he drawled as he crossed the bathroom and jumped down into the tub beside her. "Or I will be when I have time to think about it."

"It's just a little tiger," Pandora said coaxingly.

"I don't know whether I should ask where you acquired him. I have an idea that I don't want to know."

"Bazaar. Poachers," Pandora said succinctly.

"I'm sure there's considerably more to the tale than that, but I can wait until later for the details." His usually cynical eyes were still alight with laughter and a rare tenderness as he looked down into her face. "You can't keep him, you know," he said gently. "We'll have to send him to the wildlife reserve."

"I know that." Pandora's eyes were misty. "It's not fair to take away a wild thing's freedom just because we want to love and keep it close to us. It wouldn't be right."

There was an odd look on Philip's face. "No, it wouldn't be right," he repeated in an abstracted way. He glanced down at the cub in her arms and reached out to take it from her. "I'll give your friend to Raoul to care for until we can make arrangements to transport him."

"No." Pandora took a hasty step backward. "I'll take him to Raoul. He gets a little excited sometimes. He might scratch you."

His gaze was on the gauze bandage on her forearm. "So I see. I take it that's a souvenir from this harmless little baby?"

She nodded, a grimace on her face.

"Yet I'm not to be allowed to take my chances?" he asked with a curious smile.

"That's different." She shrugged. "He sort of belongs to me."

"Not so different," he said softly. He took the cub and held him gently but firmly. "*You* sort of belong to me." He turned away so that he didn't see the radiance that dawned on her face. "Get your things together. I'm sending you back to your father for the time being. I think we all agree that this punishment detail wasn't exactly a success." He had climbed the two steps of the tub and was striding toward Zilah, his expression as cynical and inscrutable as ever. "I'll be back for you in twenty minutes." He paused beside Zilah to give her a slightly crooked smile. "I still think there was magic used, Miss Dabala, but I'm not sure which one of you was the spellweaver. You must be a good deal more softhearted than most women to let Pandora talk you into this particular madness. By the way, I forgot to give you a message from Daniel." For an instant there was a touch of lingering amusement in his eyes. "I don't know how it slipped my mind. It seems three of your former captors have been apprehended, but Hassan is still at large. Daniel is waiting for a phone call with more information, so he won't be able to join you for dinner. He said he'd stop by later."

He didn't wait for a reply, and she turned from watching the door close behind him to see that Pandora hadn't moved from where Philip had left her. Her face was still wearing that expression of sunrise glory and Zilah felt a shiver of fear run through her. Pandora experienced emotions with more intensity than anyone she had ever known. How could she help but be hurt?

"Don't be so happy," Zilah whispered. "Don't let him mean so much to you, Pandora. It's not safe."

"What is safe in this world?" Pandora shrugged. "I'd rather be happy now and perhaps unhappy tomorrow than take a chance on not being happy at all. I can't live like that." She hoisted herself to the edge of the tub and got to her feet. "I have to get my things from the guest room next door. I don't want to keep Philip waiting. He may have time to reconsider and realize he's really furious about Androcles." She grinned cheerfully. "I'll see you tomorrow morning at five at the stables. Now that I'm off restriction, I'll have to find out if Oedipus has missed me."

Zilah shook her head. "Pandora, won't you ever learn? You know riding Oedipus is stupid."

The grin faded from Pandora's face and something raw and painful flared in its place. "You're the one who is stupid," she said fiercely. "You want Daniel Seifert. You have all the weapons to get him and you're not doing anything about it." Her hands clenched at her sides. "*You're* not helpless. You could do something. But you're afraid to take the chance of losing what you've got. Now, *that's* stupid."

Zilah felt she must look as stunned as Philip when he'd seen Androcles in the bathtub. Only this tigress wasn't at all cuddly and knew exactly where to strike for maximum effect.

There was a flicker of remorse on Pandora's face and she gave Zilah an awkward hug as she passed her on the way to the door. "Sorry," she muttered. "But it's true. Every bit of it is true." She opened the door. "Think about it."

There wasn't any question that she'd do

that, Zilah thought dazedly. She supposed she should be thinking about the news Philip had given her concerning Hassan, but it had barely registered. The danger and despair she had known at his hands now seemed a million miles away. The only thing that was real and pertinent was Daniel. She moved like a sleepwalker across the room to the fretted window to stare blindly out at the distant hills which were wreathed in the purple mists of dusk.

Was she afraid? Had she grabbed at the straw of friendship Daniel had extended because she so desperately wanted him to stay in her life at any cost? There was even the possibility that she did have subconscious doubts of her own self-worth, as Daniel had suggested. Had she felt she didn't deserve his love? Pandora had said he desired her. Yet, if that was true, why had he rejected her when she had offered herself this morning? Daniel was the most direct and basic of men and had no use for hypocrisy. No, Pandora must have been mistaken.

But he *had* wanted her before. That night in the cave he had wanted her with an intensity of passion that had seemed incredible. Perhaps if she tried she could make him feel like that again. But how did a woman go about tempting a man? She would probably be laughable in the role of temptress. Perhaps she'd better be content with . . .

No! She was being as cowardly as Pandora had accused her. In only a few days Daniel would probably be taking her home to Zalandan. After that, who knew when she would see him again? A mistress had a much more potent draw than a mere friend. It was better to risk rejection than to sit meekly by with her hands folded, waiting for Daniel to leave her. Surely there was something she could do that would make her more desirable in his eyes. She turned away from the window to cross to the wing chair by the bed. She sat down and leaned her head back, her expression both intent and abstracted. Pandora was right. She had a good deal of thinking to do.

Zilah didn't answer the door at the first knock. Daniel was about to knock again and then hesitated. It was after eleven. Perhaps she had given up on him and gone to bed.

Then the door swung open and Zilah was standing there. At least he hadn't gotten her out of bed. She was wearing a white satin tailored robe and her feet were bare, but there was still a light burning on the bedside table, and her eyes were alert and wide awake as she gazed up at him.

"I know it's late, but Clancy just called back. I was going to wait until morning, but I didn't want to take the chance of your worrying about it all night."

"Clancy?" she asked vaguely. Then she stepped back and away from the door. "Oh, yes, Hassan. It was very kind of you to stop by. Come in."

He hesitated. Then he entered the room and closed the door. "They weren't able to get any more information out of the others regarding Hassan's whereabouts. Clancy thinks they really don't know." He smiled grimly. "They would have spilled their guts if they had."

"That's too bad." Zilah nervously brushed a strand of hair away from her face. "Do you think he's still around here?"

"If he is, he won't get near you," he said gently. "You don't have to be frightened."

"I'm not frightened."

She *was* frightened. He had seen the slight trembling of her hand as she brushed a shining strand of hair away from her face and the quickened pulse in the hollow of her throat. He took an impulsive step forward, his hands reaching out to cup her shoulders. He could feel the warm silkiness of her skin beneath the thin robe and knew immediately that the impulse to comfort had been a mistake. He forced himself to keep his grasp light and impersonal. "He won't hurt you. I won't let him touch you. No one will touch you."

Her head bent and her hair slid forward to shadow her face. "That's what I'm afraid of," she said shakily.

"What?" He frowned in puzzlement.

She moistened her lips nervously, her lashes veiling her eyes. "I want to be touched," she said haltingly. "I want *you* to touch me, Daniel. And I'm scared to death you're not going to do it."

She heard him inhale sharply, but she didn't look up. She was afraid she would lose her courage if she did. "Pandora said that you want me." Her hands were suddenly working at the tie at her waist. "I don't know if she's right, but if you don't, I'd like you to. Oh, God, that sounds awkward. I don't know how to entice a man, dammit." The tie suddenly gave way and she opened the robe and stepped closer, pressing her soft naked body against his now rigid one. "Does this help?"

He shuddered. Every muscle had turned to stone. "Zilah, don't do this to me." He closed his eyes. "I can't take it."

"Have I embarrassed you?" she asked

miserably. "I knew Pandora was wrong, but I thought maybe I could make it work."

"Damn Pandora!" he said through clenched teeth. "I told you I didn't want any free handouts because you feel sorry for me. Of course I want you." His hips arched suddenly, bringing her into intimate contact with his hard arousal. "I've been almost wild for you ever since that night in the cave. That doesn't mean I can't control it. You don't have to be afraid of me, Zilah."

She felt a brilliant burst of joy within her. He wanted her! It wasn't everything, but it was a lot. Friendship and desire. She could build on that. "I'm not afraid," she said softly. "You keep thinking I'm some sort of hysterical ninny. Open your eyes and look at me, Daniel." He opened his eyes and met her clear, honest gaze. "Do I look afraid?" she asked softly. "Was I afraid in that cave?"

"I didn't think so at the time," he said hoarsely. "But later I thought maybe . . . I was rough with you. I lost control and went crazy."

"So did I." Her hand went up to touch his mouth. "It was like the end of the world." Her fingers traced the hard bone of his cheek. "Or the beginning. I couldn't decide which at the time." She took a step backward, the robe hanging open to reveal silken shadowy mysteries. "Do you think we could find out now?"

"Honey, I want it to be so beautiful for you," he whispered. His face was beautifully sensual. "I want to be so gentle and loving. Lately I've been lying awake at night thinking of how I would touch you. All the moves and ways I'd make it good for you." His eyes were dark and glazed with heat. "But I'm hurting so much that I don't know if I can do it."

"Then let me make it good for you." Zilah smiled lovingly. "Giving is even more beautiful than taking."

He took a deep breath. "God, you're sweet. How did I get so lucky? I'll try." His hands slid from her shoulders to her nape. "I'll try my damnedest not to take more than I give." He tilted her head up; his hands tangled in the thick length of her hair. His lips lowered slowly. Too slowly. She wanted his mouth with a wildness that shocked her. She arched into his body and pressed her lips to his with a little moan of need.

He froze. Then ice turned to flame as he groaned and took her lips with a passion that was close to savagery. He brushed and stroked back and forth against her mouth. He bit her lips and then soothed them with a warm, sensual tongue. He devoured her as if he were famished. Yet she heard him give a low groan of hunger deep in his throat, even as he feasted.

She was vaguely aware that his hands had returned to her shoulders and were pushing the white robe off her arms. It fell into a silken pool on the carpet and his hard, warm hands were moving down her spine in feverish exploration. "I'd watched you ride ahead of me on that gray mare," he muttered. He cupped her buttocks, kneading their softness in his big hands. "And I'd think what a pretty bottom you had and how much I'd like to do this."

"Did you?" She could barely get the words out. Her chest was so tight she couldn't breathe. Her breasts were crushed against the crisp cotton of his blue shirt and she could feel his heat beneath it. "I didn't realize that. I guess you thought I was pretty dumb."

"Blind," he murmured. "You had to be blind." He buried his face in the side of her throat and nuzzled the smooth flesh gently. "I couldn't even look at you without going into an erotic daydream."

"What about?" She scarcely knew what she was saying. Her head was whirling. His hands were so big and powerful yet they were cupping and squeezing her with such gentleness.

"I intend to describe every one," he assured her with a husky laugh. "Complete with demonstration." He was suddenly lifting her and rubbing her against his loins. "This is one I had often. Do you like the feel of me, Zilah?"

Her fingers were digging into his shoulders. "Oh, yes," she said faintly. Her eyes closed and her head fell languidly against his chest. His heart was throbbing hard against her ear. Very hard. "I like that daydream very much."

"No dream now. Reality." He slowly let her slide down his body inch by inch. She could feel the readiness of every muscle and tendon. Then her bare toes touched the floor and he was backing away from her. There was a slight smile on his face and his eyes were smoldering. "Reality for both of us. Have you had a few fantasies too, Zilah?"

Color flooded her cheeks. "Yes, I suppose I have." She felt so vulnerable standing there before him naked while he was fully clothed. Vulnerable and shy.

He leaned back against the door. She knew how aroused he was. Yet his pose was deceptively lazy, his shoulders resting against the door, his jean-clad legs slightly spread. The faded denim clung softly to the powerful muscles of his calves and thighs. His feet were bare except for the brown sandals he wore, and his feet looked as strong and hard as the rest of him.

"What would you like to do to me?" he asked softly. "Any way I can please you, I will. I'm at your disposal." His eyes were on her face, lingering on the wild flush that touched her cheeks and the bruised softness of her mouth. "Are you shy? Would you like me to start?"

She nodded. "I feel . . ." She shook her head helplessly. "Strange."

He smiled gently. "You won't for very long. It will all come together. Okay, my fantasy first. Walk over to the bed — slowly. I want to watch the play of the lamp light on your body and watch your hair move and shine against the naked flesh of your back."

She did as he asked. She could feel his eyes on her as she crossed the room. It was almost as if he were touching her. She could hear the sound of his breathing in the quiet room. It had roughened in the last few minutes, and she knew it was because she was arousing him. It sent a thrill of pleasure through her that dissipated the awkwardness she had been experiencing. She stopped by the bed and tossed back her hair so that it fell in a shimmering stream down her back. She glanced over her shoulder and smiled. "Like that?"

"Like that," he said thickly. "Now sit down on the bed." His eyes were still fixed on her as he took off his sandals. "Damn, you're beautiful." He was moving toward her across the room, his bare feet making no sound on the carpet. "Sleek and soft and womanly." He stopped before the spot where she was sitting on the side of the bed. "Now part your thighs." He knelt before her on the floor between her thighs. His eyes were watching her expression searchingly. "Your turn." His voice was deep and quiet in the stillness. "Here I am. What do you want from me?"

Everything. He was so close yet not brushing her with so much as a fingertip. Every nerve in her body transmitted a need that was almost painful. "I want . . . to touch you." Her tongue moistened her lips. "I want to see you. It was so dark in the cave."

"Then touch me." His smile was utterly sensual. "Look at me. I'm not as pretty as you, but what there is belongs to you." He picked up her hands and brought them to his chest. "You'll have to get rid of this shirt."

Her fingers were trembling as she unbuttoned the dark blue cotton shirt. They trembled more when he became impatient with her fumblings and decided to amuse himself by cupping and fondling her breasts in his palms. "You're so ripe and lovely." His eyes were hot and intent as he watched the pink crests spring into prominence. "Such sweet, firm cushions. Remind me to tell you about another fantasy that just came to mind."

"I can't keep up with them," she said shakily. She pushed the shirt down over his shoulders. "And I can't think when you do that."

"Good. If you can't think, then you certainly can't feel shy." He looked up, his eyes glowing softly. "Touch me, Zilah."

Her hands were trembling as she placed them flat on his chest. Hardness, heat, vitality. The cloud of red hair tickled her palms. She found his nipples in that nest and heard him gasp, and then he stiffened against her. She felt a little thrill of triumph as she slowly bent her head and licked with catlike delicacy and felt the nipple firm to hardness. His breathing was uneven but he made no other sound as she licked and even nibbled playfully for the next few minutes. It was only when she glanced up at his face that she noticed his jaw was clenched and his nostrils flared with strain. "Don't you like it?" she whispered.

His laugh held a touch of desperation. "Oh, I like it. It's just driving me crazy." He took her hand and placed it on the knotted hardness of his stomach. "See?" His arms went around her waist and he laid his cheek on her breast. "Give me a minute. I'm wanting you so much. So much." In spite of his words he was rubbing his cheek wildly against her softness as if he couldn't resist the temptation of her naked breasts. His beard was erotically abrasive against her. His lips were warm, his breath hot.

She arched, offering herself blindly. His lips captured one burgeoning nipple with desperate hunger. He was murmuring something broken and incoherent as he nibbled, sucked, ran his tongue over her in a delirium of passion. She moaned, the sound barely audible.

Then his lips were gone from her breast. They were burning the valley between her breasts, the smooth skin of her abdomen, the fleecy nest that surrounded her womanhood. He lifted his head. His eyes were blazing in his pale face. "Zilah? Say yes. I can't take much more."

She nodded. She couldn't speak. At the moment she felt utterly mindless.

He took a deep breath and tried to still the trembling that was shaking him. "You're sure? It's got to be right for you this time."

She almost laughed aloud. "I'm sure," she said shakily.

He waited no longer. He was on his feet, stripping off his clothes with an impatience that was almost savage. *He* was almost savage, she thought dazedly as her eyes ran over the tight powerful buttocks and the iron-hard sinews of his calves and thighs. He looked wild and barbaric, a naked, virile giant with flaming hair and beard.

But there was nothing savage about the dark blue eyes that were looking at her with such glowing tenderness. "Lie back," he said gently. "I won't hurt you. I'll never hurt you. We'll go slow and easy this time." He noticed her eyes on him and he smiled. "I want you. Would you like to see how much I want you? Do you want to touch me?"

She shook her head. "Not now." She smiled back at him. "Later, perhaps."

"I'll look forward to it." He pushed her down on the pillows. "Do you like my body?" He was over her, looking down at her. "Does it please you?"

"It . . . pleases me," she said haltingly. It was difficult putting words together when she was conscious only of his big hands parting her thighs and his narrowed eyes intent on her face. "You're beautiful, Daniel."

"I wasn't fishing for compliments." He smiled. "I know I'm no movie idol. I just wanted to make sure I didn't scare you. I'm such a big bastard."

He was doing it again. Why did he persist in thinking she would be frightened of him? "There's nothing frighten —"

He had entered her with one smooth plunge, taking her breath and mind and setting her body on fire. "Daniel!"

"I can't stand it," he grated. His cheeks were flushed and his eyes so beautifully sensual that she wanted to keep looking at him forever. "It's so damn *good*." He was moving slowly, carefully, filling her with himself, filling her with beauty. "We fit so well. We were meant to be together like this. Can't you feel that, love?"

She could feel *him*. She could feel the closeness and the fire and the wonder. Her hands ran over his chest, fluttering, searching mindlessly. Full, empty. Full again. Her breasts were full too, and achingly taut with the need for more of him.

She suddenly surged upward, taking more of him. He froze. His eyes closed. His chest was shuddering with the harshness of his breathing. "I wish you hadn't done that. I was doing so well. I was almost civilized." His lids flicked open. "I'm sorry. I tried."

He went wild. Stroking, plunging, moving her. His words were fevered and sweet. His hands rough, yet loving on her body. It was all bold and hot and caring. It was blinding rapture. It was Daniel. Beauty, heat, and then a flame of glory.

He collapsed in her arms, his chest moving as if he were starved for oxygen. His big fist clenched and then hit the bed with a force that shocked her. "Dammit! I blew it!"

She was so dazed that at first she was totally bewildered. "Daniel?" Her hand tangled in the soft richness of his hair, caressing, soothing.

His face was buried in her throat and she could feel him shaking against her. "I'm sorry. God, I'm sorry," he whispered. "I tried so hard. Don't hate me, Zilah."

"Hate you!" She shook her head as if to clear it. "Why should I hate you?"

"I wanted it to be beautiful for you, dammit. I wanted to be gentle and kind." He laughed. "I wanted to be a damn white knight."

"You think it wasn't beautiful for me?" She couldn't believe it. "Daniel, you're a complete idiot."

He lifted his head. "Don't try to make me feel better," he growled. "I was there, remember. I was rough as hell."

Her lips were twitching. "You're still there," she said demurely. "And you notice I'm not objecting."

"It's not funny. I don't see how you can laugh about it. I practically violated you." His lips were tight with pain. "No generosity can excuse that."

"Dammit," she said clearly. "Shut up." She framed his face with her hands and looked into his eyes. "It was beautiful. It *was* a little rough, because that's a part of you. I wouldn't have done without that part of it any more than I would the gentleness and beauty that are a part of you too." She pulled his head down and kissed him hard. "I don't know where you got the idea I was so breakable, but it's not true. Understood?"

His eyes were oddly bright. "Understood," he said gruffly. His lips covered her own with a sweetness that made her a little dizzy. He lifted his head. "All the same, I'll do better next time."

She shook her head in exasperation. Heavens, he was stubborn. Then she felt him stir within her and she smiled delightedly. "It looks like you're going to get the opportunity very soon."

"You're damn right." The rhythm began again, deep and lazy but just as thrilling. "That was one of my very favorite daydreams. Loving you." His words were punctuated with a thrusting movement that took her breath away. "And loving you. Over and over. Deeper and deeper. Sweeter and sweeter. Hotter and . . ."

She didn't know how much later it was when she felt his kiss on her temple. She was lying in perfect contentment, her head on his shoulder, watching moonlight filter through the fretted window across the room. The lamp was out now and there was only the darkness, the moonlight, and Daniel.

"Well, have you decided, old friend?" he asked softly.

"Decided?"

"Whether it's the end of the world or the beginning?"

She cuddled closer. "Oh, the beginning." Rebirth, sunrise, the world remade in his arms. "Definitely the beginning, Daniel."

9

Those blissful feelings of renaissance and warm contentment were still with her when she opened her eyes a few hours later. It was the gray hour before dawn and she was tempted to close her eyes and go back to sleep. It was so lovely to be held like this in Daniel's arms. She snuggled closer and felt those arms tighten around her in unconscious possession.

Last night had been wonderful and Daniel so loving. Even though no words of commitment had been spoken, surely their loving meant something. His words, when he had made love to her, had been of passion and possession. Still, later, when passion was spent, he had been so marvelously gentle and caring that hope had sprung into full bloom. But she mustn't ask for too much. She had been given the lovely seeds of friendship and desire. She would nourish them well and pray that they would grow into love.

The room was cool. Zilah pulled the sheet higher to cover Daniel's shoulders, careful not to wake him. She closed her eyes. Then they flicked open as a sudden memory pierced the mists of contentment. Pandora. She felt like groaning aloud. Oh, damn, it was almost dawn, and Pandora would be at the stables waiting for her.

And if she didn't go, there was every chance that Pandora would take Oedipus out again. Not that she could prevent it anyway, she thought crossly. However, there was no question that she had to try. Not only was there the possibility of Pandora being physically hurt riding the big stallion, but even if that didn't occur, Philip was sure to be angry enough to completely devastate the girl verbally.

Although he had been surprisingly indulgent with Pandora the night before, she remembered with a touch of speculation. In fact, Zilah had been astounded at the sheikh's gentleness with Pandora. There had been a rapport between them that would have been noticeable to even the most casual onlooker.

She didn't want to think about Philip or Pandora or anything but Daniel right now, dammit. If she had any sense, she would leave Pandora to her own willful pursuits and their consequences. She sighed in discouragement because even as she gave herself this very sensible advice she was cautiously removing Daniel's arm from around her and slipping out of the bed. She knew she couldn't do that. She cared about Pandora. The girl might be wild and willful, but there was an eagerness and generosity about her that were completely endearing. Zilah couldn't just ignore the fact that there was every chance Pandora would get into trouble if she wasn't there to prevent it.

Perhaps she would be back before Daniel awoke, she thought wistfully. She quickly grabbed underthings, jeans, a long-sleeved white sweatshirt, and her boots from the closet and then disappeared into the bathroom. However, with Pandora there was no telling. She'd better leave Daniel a note.

A short time later she was crossing the stableyard. The sun still hadn't risen, though there were faint lavender streaks piercing the blue-gray clouds. She loved this time of the morning when the world was so silent that she could hear her footsteps on the soft turf. It reminded her of the many times she and Jess Bradford had risen at this hour and ridden out in the predawn mornings at the ranch. There was something about the quiet and serenity of this time of day that bred a comfortable companionship, a silent joining of the spirit.

She knew at once, when she caught sight of Pandora leaning against the fence, staring blindly out into the pasture, that there would be no serene, companionable ride this morning.

Pandora was dressed in her customary riding garb of jeans and dark ribbed sweater but that was all that was usual about her. Pandora's back was to her and Zilah couldn't read the expression on her face, but it was scarcely necessary. That back was braced with a tense rigidity as if to bear some torturous strain. She could almost see the effort the girl was making to retain control.

"Pandora?"

Pandora didn't turn around. "I saddled up Dancing Lady for you. She's still in the stall. I wasn't sure when you'd be coming. I thought I'd wait around until you got here though." She laughed shakily. "I didn't want you to think I'd stood you up."

"Pandora, what's wrong?" Zilah had drawn next to the girl and was gazing searchingly at her averted face. "What's happened?"

"Nothing much." Pandora's slim, nervous hands tightened on the bars of the fence. "It's just turned out that I'm not going to be around here anymore. I'm going away this morning. Philip gave me the good news when he drove me home last night. I'm to be whisked away in Philip's helicopter to Marasef and put on a plane for England. Isn't that exciting?"

"England?" Zilah echoed, shocked. "I don't understand."

"Don't you?" Pandora asked tautly. "Philip says that the private schools in England are very good. He's sending me to his agent in London, who's going to find just the right one for me. Philip's specified that it have a fine stable and that it specialize in training Olympic equestrian candidates. Isn't that absolutely wonderful?"

"But why so suddenly? He didn't seem at all angry last night."

"You don't understand." Pandora's words were coming with feverish rapidity. "This isn't a punishment. He's only doing what's best for me. That's what he said. 'This is what's best for you, Pandora.' He kept saying that over and over. He wouldn't listen to me." One hand released the bar and balled into a fist that turned her knuckles white. "He wouldn't *listen* to me."

"What about your father? Doesn't he have anything to say about this?"

"I told you, he does anything Philip tells him to do. If Philip told him to send me to darkest Africa to make a meal for the cannibals, he would do it."

"England isn't so bad," Zilah said gently. "Perhaps this *will* be best for you. Why don't you give it a chance? Philip must have thought it was, or he wouldn't be sending you away." She felt achingly sorry for the girl. She wanted to reach out and hold her, comfort her, but that control was too fragile. It might shatter at any moment.

Pandora muttered a curse that was charged with pain. "That's not the reason he's sending me away," she said with a violence that had a touch of desperation. "I was coming too close. Philip won't let anyone come too close. He knew I'd never stop trying to make him —" She broke off and drew a deep shaky breath. "I knew that, when he was giving me all that hogwash about doing what was best for me. He just wanted to get the kid away and out of his life. He'd be safe then." She shrugged. "Maybe he doesn't even know it himself."

"Well, if you can't do anything —"

"The hell I can't!" Pandora turned to face her, and Zilah experienced a shock at the agony in the young girl's face. Agony and a relentless purpose. Her dark eyes were glowing with an almost incandescent strength. "He can send me away but he can't make my choices as to how I run my life. He can keep his wonderful school. I'll find my own way." She closed her eyes. "And it *will* be my way. I'll get over this pain," she whispered. "You'll see, I'll get over it." She opened her eyes that were glittering with unshed tears. "Good-bye, Zilah. I'll try to keep in touch."

Then she was gone. Running across the stableyard as if she were a creature of the night fleeing the dawn.

Oh, God, such pain. It didn't seem fair that she, herself, was so happy and full of hope when Pandora was so miserable. She couldn't let her go without trying to speak to her again. Perhaps Daniel could talk to Philip . . . No, that would serve no purpose. She had an idea the sheikh was an immovable object when he made up his mind. It would only put a strain on the friendship that Daniel valued so highly. If Pandora's father was in accord, there was nothing anyone could do to prevent her being sent to England. Perhaps the best thing Zilah could do would be to try to reconcile Pandora to the idea and offer her all the support she could give her.

Zilah suddenly had no desire to go riding. All she wanted to do was go back to Daniel's arms, where she felt so secure. Where she could experience again that hope she had known this morning. She had turned away and had already taken a few strides toward the house when she stopped suddenly. Dancing Lady. Pandora had said she had already saddled her. She'd have to go into the stable and unsaddle her. Her steps were quick with impatience as she crossed the stableyard and entered the shadowy stall-lined barn. Dancing Lady was in the first stall, and Zilah reached for the latch to open the wooden gate.

"I thought for a few minutes you were going to disappoint me."

She froze. Her heart stopped and then started beating again in double-time. Hassan!

He stepped out from behind a high stack of baled hay, his rifle held almost casually in the crook of his arm. "You looked as if you were undecided whether to come into the stable or not." He smiled mockingly, his dark eyes gleaming in the dim light. "That would have been a pity. I was getting tired of my long vigil. I've been here almost twenty-four hours, you know. I was even tempted to take the little silver-haired girl as hostage when she came in this morning to saddle the mare. I stopped only because I didn't know who she was. After waiting so long I didn't want to waste my valuable time on a nobody."

"How did you know I was here?" Zilah asked jerkily.

"This is a very small world and the sheikh and his guests are of prominent interest to the residents. I asked a few discreet questions in the bazaar." His hand tightened on the stock of the rifle. "I listened and I watched. I even saw you and Seifert at a distance on one of your early morning rides a few days ago. Did you know this rifle has a telescopic sight?" His palm rubbed the wood caressingly. "I can't tell you how close I was to killing Seifert. But it wouldn't have done me any good to kill him if you got away. Then they would have gotten scared and moved you to Zalandan right away."

"You still think you can get away with holding me hostage?" Zilah shook her head. "It didn't work last time." She lifted her chin. "Daniel made fools of you and your men."

"He caught us off guard," Hassan snarled. "It won't happen again." A wavering ray of light flickered into the dimness and she could see him more clearly. The sight wasn't encouraging. He looked wild, desperate, and very deadly. His madras shirt and black pants were dirty and stained and he had a dark stubble on his thin cheeks.

"They've already caught the other three men and they'll catch you too." Hassan had stiffened at her words. "You didn't know that, did you? They caught them yesterday morning."

"They were cowards and fools. They gave up before the game was half played." Hassan's lips twisted. "Now that I have you, the game begins again with a brand new deck of cards. This time I'll have to think of something to do to you to convince Ben Raschid that the game is to be played in earnest."

Zilah felt a chill of terror run down her spine. "But you don't have me." She tried to keep her voice steady. "How do you expect to get me away from the compound? Someone is sure to see you."

"Then they'll also see the gun at your back." He smiled faintly. "And I doubt if they'll interfere."

"Zilah, I'm glad I caught you," Daniel said as he entered the stable. He was grinning and his voice was light and teasing. "What the devil do you mean running out —" He broke off as he saw the tenseness in her figure.

He stiffened, his body automatically tautening with the instinct of a jungle animal sensing danger. Then his gaze discovered the threatening figure in the deeper shadows to the left of the door. He uttered a low, violent curse.

"Ah, our special envoy, Mr. Seifert," Hassan said silkily. "This is an unexpected pleasure. I thought I was going to have to demand your head as part of the ransom of my brother, but now that won't be necessary."

"You're a fool, Hassan. Clancy Donahue has half the agents on the security team scouring the province for you. You'll never get away with it," Daniel said roughly. "If you're smart, you'll run like hell and only hope it's fast enough."

"I don't give up that easily. My brother is rotting in that tyrant's prison in Marasef." Hassan's eyes were flickering wildly in his taut face. "The others may give in, but I will not." He gestured with the rifle. "Get away from that door."

Daniel hesitated and then moved slowly to stand beside Zilah at the stall. He watched with narrowed eyes while Hassan edged sidewise until he was standing in

250

front of the open stable door facing them.

Hassan smiled with satisfaction. "Now, come along, my pretty whore, we have a long way to go."

Daniel took an impulsive step forward and then stopped as the barrel of the rifle lifted. "I'm going to kill you." Daniel's voice was deadly certain. "I hope you know that, Hassan. You're building your own funeral pyre, stick by stick."

"Am I?" A mocking smile touched Hassan's lips again. "I seem to have drawn blood. Is it possible you feel something more than responsibility for the pretty lady? I've heard that some men form sentimental attachments to prostitutes on occasion, but I thought you were a man of discrimination."

"Hassan . . ." Daniel grated warningly between set teeth.

"Did she tell you about the House of the Yellow Door?" Hassan taunted. "She wasn't even a khadim, just a common wh — Take another step and I'll put a bullet hole through the center of your forehead. I gather you didn't know about the lady's past."

"I knew."

Zilah felt a galvanic shock that was more traumatic than the one that had shaken her

251

when she first saw Hassan. Her eyes flew to Daniel's set face. He had known all along! But if that were true, why hadn't he told her?

Hassan's brow rose. "Yet still so protective? She must be very good. I'll have to sample her myself while she's in my . . . care."

"Stick by stick," Daniel repeated coldly. "And it will be very painful, Hassan."

"But you won't be around to light that pyre." Hassan's finger tightened on the trigger. "Will you, Seifert?"

"No!" Zilah took an impulsive step forward. "Don't hurt him. I'm the one you want. Killing Daniel won't help free your brother. If you won't hurt him, I'll come with you without a struggle."

"Shut up, Zilah," Daniel said hoarsely.

"See how eager she is to try a new man?" Hassan's lips curved in a smug smile. "You'll do anything I want, won't you, pretty lady?"

"Yes, anything," Zilah whispered. "Please, don't kill him."

Daniel's face was drawn and haggard with pain. "For God's sake, Zilah, can't you see he's just —"

There was a sudden blur of movement and the rifle went off.

"Daniel!" Zilah wasn't even aware that she had screamed. But the bullet hadn't hit Daniel. It had ricocheted off the post beside them. The blur of movement had been Pandora bolting through the door and grabbing the rifle. She was now hanging on to Hassan like a ferocious little mongoose on a cobra. Then Daniel was across the yards separating them, ripping the gun from Hassan's grip with one hand and giving him a powerful karate blow on the neck with the other.

Hassan didn't make a sound as he slumped to the ground.

It was all over. It had happened so fast, Zilah felt slightly dazed. Daniel was safe. She felt such a surge of thanksgiving that her knees were shaking. She slowly crossed to where Daniel was stripping off his belt. He flipped the unconscious Hassan over on his stomach. "Are you all right?" he asked curtly. "He didn't hurt you before I got here?"

"No, I'm fine. I was here for only a few minutes with him. Before that I was in the stableyard with Pandora." She turned to Pandora, who was picking herself up off the floor and brushing hay and sawdust off her jeans. "Why did you come back? Not that I wasn't extremely glad to see you."

Pandora shrugged. "I didn't say good-bye to Oedipus. I couldn't leave without doing that. Then I saw that slime" — she gestured to Hassan — "pointing his gun at you. So I jumped him."

"And quite efficiently too," Daniel said with a grin. "If you ever need a job, remind me to give you a first-class recommendation to Clancy Donahue."

"You could have been killed," Zilah said.

"I wasn't," Pandora said simply. "No use looking back at might-have-beens."

It was almost as if it were Daniel speaking. Their philosophies were so similar. Practical, direct, honest.

Honest? Zilah felt an aftershock go through her as she remembered Daniel's admission that he had known about her past. Known and not told her that he had known.

"When did you find out about the House of the Yellow Door?" she whispered.

He didn't glance up from strapping Hassan's hands behind his back with a belt. "When you had the fever," he said absently. "You said something and I put Clancy through the third degree."

"Clancy told you," she repeated numbly. "Of course, Clancy knew everything. He was there." She folded her arms across her breasts. She was suddenly shivering. When hope died, it did that to you, she thought dully. It turned the whole world into ice. "Why didn't you tell me?"

"I thought it best not to." He glanced up and saw the expression on her face. He suddenly stiffened warily. "It wasn't important anyway."

"Wasn't it?" Her voice was strained. "I think it was. I think it was very important. If I'd known, I never would have pushed as I did last night. You must have been very embarrassed. I'm sorry I put you in that position."

"What the hell are you talking about?" Daniel said roughly. "You're not making any sense."

"I think we both know what I'm talking about." Her voice broke. She mustn't let go. She had to be strong. "I understood perfectly, Daniel. You don't have to pretend any longer."

"Pretend? Dammit, Zilah. I don't even know what you're hinting at."

The tears were suddenly racing down her cheeks. "Stop it! Do you hear me? Stop it! I won't be pitied." She turned and was running out the door. "I don't need it. I won't be pit —" She couldn't speak anymore. The sobs were shaking her body as she tore across the stableyard. She had to be alone. She had to go somewhere to hide, to lick her wounds and gain control again. She couldn't face Daniel again until she did. Poor Daniel. He had been so kind. Why hadn't she let well enough alone and not thrown herself at him last night? Now she had probably lost a friend as well as a lover. She climbed the fence and dropped down into the pasture. Then she was running wildly across the meadow toward the tamarisk trees and the poppy field that lay beyond.

Pandora turned away from the door. "She's running across the pasture," she said fiercely. "Why aren't you going after her? She was crying, dammit."

Daniel gave her a glance that was just as fierce. "Do you think I don't want to? Am I supposed to leave Hassan for you to handle by yourself?"

"Is that all?" Pandora picked up the rifle from the floor, went back out into the stableyard, and fired four shots into the air in rapid succession. "That should bring someone running." She turned and strode briskly back into the barn. She sat down cross-legged on the floor with the rifle barrel pressed to Hassan's head. "Get going."

Daniel stared at her in astonishment. Then

a slow grin lit his face. "Well, I'll be damned." He stood up. "A recommendation. Anytime. You're quite a woman, Pandora."

She shook her head, her lips curving in a bittersweet smile. "I'm just a kid who doesn't know what's good for her. I have it on the best authority. Now, get going. Dancing Lady is already saddled."

He gave her a half salute before crossing the stable and opening the stall gate. He led the mare to the double doors that led to the stableyard. He hesitated, not entirely sure that he should leave. Then he sighted two grooms running toward them across the stableyard and breathed a sigh of relief. Pandora should be perfectly safe now.

His lips tightened grimly. He only hoped Zilah would be equally safe. She had been crying so hard she must have been almost blinded by tears. Who knew what kind of trouble she could fall into? He swung into the saddle and cantered toward the pasture gate.

10

Zilah had nearly reached the meadow of wild poppies when she heard the hoofbeats. She didn't halt or look behind her even when she heard Daniel shouting her name.

Then he was almost on top of her. "Zilah, if you don't stop, I'm going to have to try to scoop you up like one of those blasted movie heros. You know what a lousy rider I am. We'll probably both end up in the dirt on our asses."

"Go away. I can't talk now." Her voice was still unsteady though the sobs that had shaken her had finally ceased. "I'll see you later. I want to be alone."

"The hell you do," Daniel said grimly. "You can just cut out the Garbo bit. There's no way I'm going to let you out of my sight until we get this straightened out. Now, are you going to stop or do I scoop?"

"Daniel, I . . ." He'd do it. She knew he would. She had seen that bulldog tenacity in action before. Oh, God, she wasn't going to be able to bear this. She stopped, trying desperately to maintain her delicately balanced control. "Please go away, Daniel."

He had reined in Dancing Lady and was swinging off the mare. "I can't do that," he said simply. "Any more than I can let you go. Ask me anything but that."

"Your responsibility is over. Hassan has been captured. I'm well again. There's no reason for you to pretend any longer."

"Pretend!" His hand grasped her shoulders and he gave her a shake. His eyes were blazing in his white face. "I don't know how to play games like that. I never learned. I don't want to learn."

"You played a fairly intricate one with me," she said. "You're obviously not as amateurish at it as you'd have me believe." She shook her head wearily. "I don't want to argue. It doesn't solve anything. I understand why you had to keep me here, Daniel, and I'm not blaming you. You told me Alex Ben Raschid wanted the terrorists. It was very clever of you to use me as a decoy."

"Decoy? You think I kept you here as a lure for Hassan and his men?"

"Pandora said there was no medical reason for me to be here." Zilah's eyes were fixed on the top button of his shirt. She would *not* start weeping again. "You made the last ten days very pleasurable for me. I'm only sorry I forced you into that situation last night. I didn't understand."

Daniel uttered a round of unprintable words that caused her eyes to lift swiftly to his face.

"Come on." He led her a few paces away from the mare. "Sit down. This may take a while. I've never heard such a bunch of bull in my life." His hands on her shoulders forced her to her knees. He knelt beside her. "Now, I'm going to take this point by point and try to pound some sense into your head. It's either that or I'm going to go bananas. First, why do you think I wanted you here to use you as bait? Didn't it ever occur to you there could be another reason?"

"What other reason could there be?" Zilah was staring blindly over his shoulder. "It was a very clever move. Clancy must be pleased with you."

"For your information, Clancy threatened to nail my ass for keeping you here."

"He didn't agree with your plan?" she asked dully. "Well, you proved him wrong, didn't you?"

"There wasn't a plan, dammit." His voice was as exasperated as his expression. "I didn't have any plan but keeping you with me as long as I could get away with it."

"You don't have to spare my feelings. I know you don't feel anything for me but friendship. You've never behaved as anything other than a very kind older brother all the time I've been here." Her lips tightened with pain. "Until I forced myself on you last night."

"I think one of us is going crazy." Daniel's expression was stunned. "For God's sake, look at me. I'm twice your size and weight. You're speaking as if you held me down and raped me. I wasn't exactly fighting you off, was I?"

She shook her head miserably. "You were very kind. You're always ki —"

"Kind!" It was almost a roar. "Are you blind? I went out of my head loving you last night. I get excited just looking at you. I've been one big ache for the last ten days."

Her eyes widened uncertainly. "Is that true? Then why have you been so . . ."

"Because when you had that fever you looked at me as if I were some kind of monster. It scared the hell out of me." His lips were a flat line of remembered pain. "I couldn't risk your ever looking at me like that again. It hurt too damn much."

"You felt sorry for me," she whispered.

His breath released explosively. "Okay, let's go into that question of pity. The very idea seems to blow you sky high. You're damned right I pity you."

"Well, you can stop right now." She lifted her chin. "I don't want your pity any more than you wanted mine that night in the cave."

"I can't cut it off just because you don't want it," he said. "It exists. It nearly ripped my heart out when I heard what happened to you. I wanted to commit murder. Then I wanted to pick you up and put you in a glass case, where no one could ever hurt you again." His hands tightened on her shoulders. "No, not a glass case. I wanted to create a brand new world for you. A world where there was only sunshine and flowers. A place where children would never know pain or hunger or any of the twisted horrors that you did." His eyes were glistening as they looked into her own. "But I can't do that. I have to accept the world just as you do. I can only try to protect and care for you now. To make your world as beautiful as I can today and tomorrow." He shook his head. "But don't ask me not to pity you, or at least the child you were, Zilah."

"Will you stop talking about it!" The tears were running down her cheeks again. "I never wanted that. There's only one thing I ever wanted from you."

He went still. "And what's that, Zilah?"

"Never mind." She tried to shrug his hands from her shoulders. "I don't want to talk anymore. Please, let me go, Daniel."

His grip tightened, quelling her resistance. "What did you want from me, Zilah?"

"I wanted you to love me," she burst out. "Wasn't that stupid? I wanted your love, not your damn pity."

His expression was stunned. "What the hell are you talking about? Of course I love you. What do you think all this means?"

"I know you care about me as a friend," she said huskily. "I want more. I tried to be satisfied with the other, but it's not enough."

"Lord, you're muddle-headed." His hands left her shoulders and moved up to frame her face. His exasperation was suddenly gone and his expression held such exquisite tenderness that it caused her heart to flutter. "Listen carefully. I will love you as a friend, as a mistress, and as the mother of my future children. I will love you through rain and storm and sunshine. I will love you through peace and war and everything in between. I've loved you for so long that it seems forever, and I will love you beyond forever." He smiled gently. "Is that clear, love?"

Her eyes were misty and uncertain. "Truly?"

"Truly." He shook his head ruefully. "How could I help but love you? You're everything any man could want. Why the hell do you persist in doubting it? You're quite a woman, Zilah Dabala."

Joy was beginning to spread tentative golden tendrils through her. Daniel loved her. It was too wonderful to believe. Yet how could she help believing when he was looking at her like that? "I know I am." She smiled shakily. "Only, sometimes, I forget."

"Why do you forget?" Daniel asked, his expression grave and intent. "Why, Zilah?"

She bit her lip. "It's part of what happened to me I guess." She shrugged. "In spite of all the psychiatrist's soothing words, there are times when I still feel the dirtiness." She paused. "And the guilt."

"Guilt?" he asked, astonished. "For God's sake, you were a victim. An innocent victim of an atrocious crime. Would you feel guilt if you had been shot or stabbed?"

She smiled a little sadly. "But you see, it's the very nature of the crime that instills the guilt. I know it's unreasonable. I don't know whether it's a reflection of society's attitude or some holdover from a time when women preferred 'death before dishonor.' " She looked up at him soberly. "You say you love me, but can you honestly say that you wouldn't rather I had been wounded by a bullet than forced to spend six months at the House of the Yellow Door?"

"You're damn right I can." He was silent a moment as if searching for words. "No, that's not true." She inhaled sharply as if he'd struck her. "Dammit, don't look like that. I didn't mean that I looked on your experience as any personal affront to me. I only meant that a bullet wouldn't have left an open festering wound as this has done. That it might have been easier for *you*. Not because of any so-called stigma."

"But then, you're an extraordinary man, Daniel." She shook her head. "I've had to accept the fact that a good many people don't feel the way you do."

"Then they're fools," Daniel said harshly. "And so are you if you pay any attention to them." He kissed her with a gentleness that was as beautiful as his words were rough. Joy again, blossoming, growing. She could almost accept it. He lifted his head, and when he spoke his voice was no longer harsh. It was deep and uneven and it rang with absolute truth. "Why should I find anything repulsive in what happened to you other than the pain itself? That experience is part of what made you what you are today. Do you know something? There's no question that I would have loved the girl you might have been without that experience. But, somehow, I'm not sure I would have loved her as much. You're stronger, deeper, wiser for what happened to you. It may have hurt you, but it also made you more gentle and sensitive to other people's pain." He had to stop for a moment before he could go on. "Do you remember what you told me about the poppy and how you had learned to accept the knowledge that it could also bring darkness and pain?"

She nodded slowly.

"You're like that poppy, Zilah. The stream of darkness only served to make you more hardy to endure the buffeting of the winds. It only made your blossoms brighter and more beautiful."

Her heart was so full that for a time she couldn't speak. He had said that he wasn't like David Bradford, but in that moment it was as if David were speaking. How lucky she was to have two such men in her life. "You do love me." There was a touch of wonder in her voice. Then as he frowned she held up her hand and grinned. "Sorry.

You're right. I'm positively wonderful. I deserve to have everyone in the whole cockeyed world love me." Her voice dropped to a whisper. "But oh, I'm so glad that *you* do. Is it all right if I say that?"

"As long as you accompany it with a little declaration of your own," he said gruffly. "I have a few insecurities myself."

Her expression was stricken. "Oh, Lord, I didn't say it, did I? But you had to know. I practically threw myself at you last night."

"Women, on occasion, have been known to crave my irresistible physique without being in love with me." His dark blue eyes were twinkling. "Not many, you understand. I can count them on one —"

He broke off as she flew into his arms. "I love you." Her arms were hugging him with a force that took his breath. "I love you so much. I never thought I could love anyone the way I do you, Daniel. I've loved you ever since you tore off that silly false ear on the plane and threw it at Hassan." Her lips were brushing swift, frantic kisses over his throat, his bearded cheeks, his ears. "Sometimes I thought I couldn't stand it when you were being so platonic. Not that it wasn't beautiful too, but . . ."

"Okay. Okay." He was chuckling, but as he pushed her away she could see that his eyes were suspiciously bright. "When you make a declaration, you don't spare the horses." He kissed the tip of her nose. "And I thought I did the platonic bit very well, considering I was going through the fires of hell trying to keep you on a pedestal and out of my bed."

"Pedestal." Her smile faded slightly. "I have an idea we've been having a massive communication breakdown." Her face was suddenly thoughtful. "I have no use for that glass case you wanted to put me in, Daniel. I don't melt in the rain and I don't break with a little rough handling. In spite of all your fine words about how strong I am, I don't think you really understand that. I've had years of being looked after as though I were so fragile that a breath would blow me away. It was all done for the best of reasons and perhaps I needed it at first." She shook her head. "But not now. You've been whipping yourself because you thought you were so rough and selfish with me that night in the cave." She touched his lips with a trembling finger. "Don't you realize how I treasured that night? You were everything that was strong and true, and yet you needed me. You didn't take anything from me that night. I gave and it was wonderful. I want to keep on giving." Her words were just above a whisper. "Don't shut me away in your dream world of sunshine and flowers. I want to live in the real world. Because that's where you live, Daniel. And I couldn't live in a world without you, no matter how beautiful it was."

"The real world," he agreed huskily. "For the rest of our lives. But don't be too generous with your giving, love. I may take too much. I've never needed anyone this much before. I'm not sure I know how to handle it."

She pulled his head down to kiss him with loving tenderness. "I'll handle —" She broke off and slowly shook her head. "No, *we'll* handle it. Together." She smiled at him. It was the summer smile he loved so much. Wise and warm with the sweet promise of joy and fulfillment to come.

A gust of wind stirred. It touched their cheeks with fresh coolness and brought with it the intoxicating scent of poppies and wild grass . . . and a sunrise world newly reborn from the darkness.

ABOUT THE AUTHOR

Iris Johansen, who has more than twenty-seven million copies of her books in print, has won many awards for her achievements in writing. The bestselling author of *Stalemate, Killer Dreams, Blind Alley, Firestorm, Fatal Tide, Dead Aim, Body of Lies,* and many other novels, she lives near Atlanta, Georgia, where she is currently at work on a new novel.

We hope you have enjoyed this Large Print book. Other Thorndike, Wheeler, and Chivers Press Large Print books are available at your library or directly from the publishers.

For information about current and upcoming titles, please call or write, without obligation, to:

Publisher
Thorndike Press
295 Kennedy Memorial Drive
Waterville, ME 04901
Tel. (800) 223-1244

or visit our Web site at:

www.gale.com/thorndike
www.gale.com/wheeler

OR

Chivers Large Print
published by BBC Audiobooks Ltd
St James House, The Square
Lower Bristol Road
Bath BA2 3SB
England
Tel. +44(0) 800 136919
email: bbcaudiobooks@bbc.co.uk
www.bbcaudiobooks.co.uk

All our Large Print titles are designed for easy reading, and all our books are made to last.